c

"I need you, Dani."

Oh, boy. He was talking about the baby. She knew that. But for a moment, she could almost imagine him meaning that in another way.

This was all about the baby, she reminded herself. So why the heated attraction?

She tried to conjure a platonic expression. "Okay. For a few days. Just long enough for you to hire someone else."

His eyes locked on hers, and a smile spread across his face, turning her tummy inside out. "You won't regret this."

Clay Callaghan might be forceful and determined. But she was, too. She'd make sure he bonded with that child, then she'd pack up the kids and take them home.

It would be a walk in the park, she told herself.

But when he gave her hand a squeeze, setting off a flurry of butterflies deep in her feminine core, she wasn't so sure about anything anymore.

Dear Reader,

I'm not sure how the months pass so quickly, but it's October again, and the holidays are fast approaching. It's easy to get caught up in the hustle and bustle of shopping, baking and decorating, not to mention the stress, but in the midst of it all, I hope you stop to count your blessings and to cherish the family in which you belong—whether you're related by blood or created by love.

It's also a time for reconciliation and renewal, for telling people you love them and offering long-overdue forgiveness.

In *Rock-A-Bye Rancher,* Clay and Dani create a family of their own and find love in the process.

If you're facing the holidays alone, I encourage you to reach out to others through your church, synagogue or community service organizations. There are a lot of lonely people in the world, and this time is especially difficult for them.

May God richly bless you and your family this year!

Judy Duarte

ROCK-A-BYE RANCHER

JUDY DUARTE

Silhouette®

SPECIAL EDITION®

Published by Silhouette Books

America's Publisher of Contemporary Romance

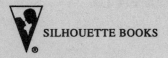 SILHOUETTE BOOKS

ISBN-13: 978-0-373-24784-4
ISBN-10:   0-373-24784-2

ROCK-A-BYE RANCHER

Copyright © 2006 by Judy Duarte

Visit Silhouette Books at www.eHarlequin.com

Printed in U.S.A.

Books by Judy Duarte

JUDY DUARTE

always knew there was a book inside her, but since English was her least favorite subject in school, she never considered herself a writer. An avid reader who enjoys a happy ending, Judy couldn't shake the dream of creating a book of her own.

Her dream became a reality in March of 2002, when the Silhouette Special Edition line released her first book, *Cowboy Courage*. Since then, she has sold nineteen more novels. Her stories have touched the hearts of readers around the world. And in July of 2005, Judy won the prestigious Reader's Choice Award for *The Rich Man's Son*.

Judy makes her home near the beach in Southern California. When she's not cooped up in her writing cave, she's spending time with her somewhat enormous, but delightfully close family. You can write to Judy c/o Silhouette Books, 233 Broadway, Suite 1001, New York, NY 10279. You can also contact her at JudyDuarte@sbcglobal.net or through her Web site—www.judyduarte.com.

To the best critique partners in the world,
Crystal Green and Sheri WhiteFeather.

Words can not express my appreciation.

Prologue

Rio Seco, Mexico

"*Pobrecita.*" Padre Luis Fernando clucked his tongue and shook his head at the solemn-faced baby girl lying in a rustic, hand-woven basket. "Three months old and no name. But don't worry, little one. I'll find someone to take you home, someone to love you."

The old priest reached out a gnarled hand to the child, waiting for her to latch on to his finger, to grasp the hope he offered. But the little girl merely lay there, lost, alone.

An hour ago one of the altar boys had come to

him in confidence, mentioning the orphaned baby and the bitter, old woman who'd been caring for her.

"Padre," the boy had said, "the church must do something. That baby isn't safe."

Manuela Vargas, a craggy-faced widow who donned dark clothing and lived alone, was considered *loca* by some of the other parishioners. And the children who lived in the community often called her *la bruja,* the witch.

Luis believed they were referring to her appearance and demeanor more than anything. Yet he had to admit that when he'd learned of the mother's death he'd been a little uneasy knowing the baby would be living with a woman who rarely smiled or interacted with the community. He'd hoped the baby would be good for her, but maybe he'd been wrong.

In a hushed tone, the boy had told him, "Manuela said that God punished Catalina for her sins and let her die giving birth. She said the baby should have died, too."

The padre hadn't needed to hear more. He'd immediately gone to visit Manuela. When he'd seen the condition of the baby, he'd convinced the old woman to give the child to him.

There had been no argument. Manuela had placed the baby girl, as well as the personal effects of the girl's mother, into the basket and gratefully passed her burden to the priest.

Luis wished he'd stepped in sooner. If he had, perhaps the young mother might still be alive.

Catalina Villa, a college student from a village nearly one hundred kilometers to the south, had shamed her family by getting pregnant. Embarrassed by her condition because she was unmarried, they had wanted her to bear her child in secret. So she was sent to live with her grandmother's sister, Manuela.

But considering Manuela's attitude about sin and punishment, Luis wondered whether a midwife or doctor had even been called when Catalina's labor started. Of course, there were some things only God knew.

The funeral had been solemn and private, with only Manuela and the baby in attendance. And sadly, the only one who had cried had been the infant.

The padre reached inside the basket that served as a crib and withdrew the prayer book that had been tucked inside. He opened to the page where the young mother had written the birth date and parentage of her child.

Catalina, he suspected, had died before entering the child's name. If she'd uttered it to anyone, Manuela had not said.

He unfolded a sheet of paper, the start of a letter:

Dear Mr. Callaghan
    You do not know me, but I loved your son

Trevor very much. When he died, I did not think I could live without him. And when I learned I was carrying his baby, I was both pleased and saddened.

My parents are very strict and believe that I have failed them. They have sent me away in shame. So I write to ask if my baby and I can come to Texas and live on the ranch with you.

I know you and Trevor were not very close, but if you can find it in your heart to accept us into your family…

The letter was unfinished, unsigned.

The priest whispered a prayer for the mother who'd died, leaving her child at the mercy of a woman with a cold and bitter heart. Then he let out a pent-up sigh and studied the fair-skinned baby girl with a head of dark, downy hair. Her cheeks lacked that rosy, healthy hue one expected to see. And her eyes, a golden brown, showed no spark of life. No hint of love.

He surmised she'd been provided with an occasional bottle of goat's milk, but nothing else. No warm embrace. No whispered words of love. Perhaps her father's relatives would be more welcoming than her mother's.

He picked up the telephone.

Twenty minutes and several calls later, he located Clay Callaghan at a ranch outside of Houston. A woman answered. Her clipped, professional tone suggested she was a servant of some kind. Luis introduced himself as a priest from a small village near Guadalajara, then asked to speak to Mr. Callaghan.

While he waited for the woman to summon the rancher, Luis again glanced at the basket and was glad to see the baby girl had fallen asleep. The sadness in her eyes haunted him in a way no other child's had.

"Por favor, Dios," the padre prayed. "Touch Señor Callaghan's heart. This baby needs someone to love her, to bond with her. She needs a home."

A deep, baritone voice sounded over a crackling telephone line. "This is Clay Callaghan."

"Señor...sir, I am Father Luis Fernando, a priest from Rio Seco, a small village outside of Guadalajara. One of my parishioners gave me an orphaned baby girl. I have reason to believe her father was Trevor Callaghan."

The line seemed to have gone dead.

"Sir? Señor Callaghan? Did you hear me?"

"Trevor died in a car accident nearly a year ago," the man responded.

"Sí. I am aware of that. In Mexico, while attending the university in Guadalajara, no? But before his death, he and a young woman named Catalina Villa Montez conceived a baby. From what I understand, they planned to marry. But your son died before they could say the vows."

"What about the child's mother?" the American asked, his curiosity validating his interest.

The padre quietly released the breath he'd been holding. "Catalina was a bright young woman from a poor village. The townspeople and her parents pooled their money to send her to the university, in hope that she would return with an education and help the community. But when her family learned she was pregnant, they were angry and embarrassed. They sent her secretly to Rio Seco, where she bore her baby in the home of a distant relative. With your son dead, *señor,* I believe she feared there were no other options."

"You said the baby was orphaned."

"*Sí.* Catalina died after childbirth and left the newborn in the care of an elderly aunt who cannot keep the baby any longer. If you will not take the baby girl to live with you in Texas, I will be forced to deliver her to an orphanage."

Silence filled the line, then the deep, graveled voice asked, "How do you know my son is the father?"

"There are blood tests that can prove it, but I was given the mother's personal effects, including a photograph of the baby's father, a handsome, blond-haired young man standing next to an airplane. I also have an engraved, black onyx ring."

Again silence. Then a graveled clearing of the throat. "Where can I find the baby?"

The padre gave him directions from the airport in Guadalajara to the church.

Surely, the American grandfather would be more loving than the old Mexican caretaker had been.

The padre prayed that he would.

Chapter One

Daniela de la Cruz sat in her seventh-floor office in Houston, Texas, gripping the telephone until her knuckles ached.

"It's not fair," her fourteen-year-old sister complained to her over the phone. "I hate being cooped up in the house, babysitting, when all my friends have the whole summer to do whatever they want and have fun."

Life *isn't* fair, Dani wanted to snap back. Deal with it, Sara. I've had to.

At twenty-five, Dani was the youngest and newest associate of Phillips, Crowley and Norman, and she was working her tail off to build a career and make a name for herself. On the outside, it appeared as though the sky was the limit in terms of her upward mobility. But that wasn't the case. Most attorneys in her position didn't have to balance home and career the way she did.

"Marcos!" Sara shrieked at her brother, obviously not covering the mouthpiece. "Put that down. You're going to break the lamp."

Dani pinched the bridge of her nose, hoping to ward off the headache that began the moment Sara called. "What's your brother doing?"

"He's swinging a baseball bat in the house," Sara said. "And he better take it outside *right now,* or I'm going to scream."

"Sara's *mean,*" the ten-year-old boy shouted in the background. "I *hate* being stuck with a couple of dumb girls."

"I'm not *dumb,*" little Delia said loud enough to be heard through the receiver.

If Dani wasn't at work and trying desperately to keep her turbulent home situation a secret, she'd pitch a fit that would rival any of Sara's.

Couldn't the teenager understand that Dani was trying her best to keep the kids fed, clothed and safe? Didn't she understand that they all had to pull together?

Dani's frustration level was at an all-time high, and she was beginning to feel inept when it came to solving the domestic disputes that were popping up regularly, now that it was summer and the kids were out of school.

Before she could respond to her squabbling brood, the intercom buzzed.

"Hang on," she told her sister.

As the teenager continued to object to the unfairness of life, Dani silenced her with the punch of the hold button. Then she tried to morph into the career-minded attorney she'd professed to be during the job-interview process and connected with the senior partner who wanted to talk to her.

"Yes, Martin."

"Daniela, can you please come into my office?"

"Certainly. I'll just be a moment." She switched lines, reconnecting with her teenage sister, who was still in mid-rant and hadn't realized she'd been on hold.

"…and all my friends are going to the mall. But oh, no. Not me. I'm stuck here at the house babysitting a bunch of juvenile ingrates."

Dani slowly shook her head and blew out an exasperated sigh. If anyone could relate to Sara's complaints, it was Dani, who'd begun looking after her younger brother and sisters after her stepmother died. When her father passed away nearly two years ago, she'd really had to step up to the plate, accepting the role of single parent. There'd never been a question about what to do with the children. She'd taken custody and tried her best to make a home for them. Her only problem had come in learning how to balance it all.

Dani had been in her third year of law school and had almost dropped out to put the family back together again, but a professor had talked her out of it.

Somehow she'd pulled it off and had passed the bar.

She loved the kids, but now that she was on a partnership track, parenting them was proving to be more difficult each day.

"Listen," she told her sister. "I'll see what I can do about lining up someone to help with child care this summer. But right now, I need you to hang in there with me. I can't come home and settle things in person, but I'll try and leave work early today. Maybe I can take Marcos and Delia to dinner and a movie. Then you can have some time with your friends, okay? It's the best that I can do."

"Well, what am I supposed to do about Marcos right now?" Sara asked. "He's driving me crazy with that baseball bat."

"Let me talk to him."

When her ten-year-old brother answered the telephone, his aggravation came out loud and clear in the tone of his voice.

"Listen up," Dani said, proceeding to make a deal with him to take him out this evening if he behaved himself.

Enthusiasm chased away his frustration. "Okay, I'll go outside and play. But can we see *Revenge of the Zombies?*"

"That's not a movie I want Delia to see," Dani said. Actually, she didn't want Marcos to see it, either. And God knew *she* didn't want to sit through it.

"But the deal is off if we have to see one of those dumb princess cartoons," he said.

Dani hated negotiating with a ten-year-old, but time and her options were running out. "I'll find something we'll all enjoy. Now take that bat outside and stop harassing the girls."

"All right."

When the line disconnected, Dani blew out an exaggerated sigh. She may have settled the dispute, at least temporarily, but she had a feeling there would be another crisis on the home front before the day was done.

She stood, tugged at her skirt, checked to see that her blouse was tucked in, then adjusted her jacket.

One of these days she feared the transformation from frenzied guardian to competent professional would fail and she'd be exposed as the phony she was—at least when it came to running a household.

For as long as she could remember, she'd wanted to be an attorney. And now that she'd made it, she wanted to excel in her new career. But something always interfered.

Something at home.

Get your mind back on work, she told herself as she entered Martin's office.

Her boss wasn't alone. Seated in front of his desk was a rugged, dark-haired man who looked to be in his forties, although it was hard to say for sure.

He was a big man, with broad shoulders and an imposing air. Instead of the typical garb of another attorney or most of their clients, he sported western wear—expensive black boots, denim jeans, a hand-tooled leather belt, a crisply pressed white shirt. Even seated, there was something commanding about him, something that drew her attention in a way that was more than professional curiosity.

He stood when she entered, and his presence seemed to take up the entire room.

"Clay," Martin said to the client, "this is Daniela de la Cruz, our newest attorney. Don't let her youth fool you. She's a real go-getter." Then he looked at Dani and grinned. "Daniela, this is Clay Callaghan. The firm handles all his legal affairs."

Dani had never met Mr. Callaghan before, but from the first day she was handed a key to the front door, she'd made it a point to learn all she could about the firm's major clients. Clay Callaghan was one of them.

He owned an impressive cattle ranch and was involved in several other business ventures—all successful and thriving. However, this denim-clad

cowboy didn't look at all like the successful businessman she'd imagined. No fancy suit, no flashy smile.
Instead, he reminded her of a Marlboro man. An outdoorsman who would be uncomfortable in a board-
room.

Yet it was she who was caught off guard, unbalanced by his presence.

As he reached out a hand to greet her, stunning
eyes, the color of a mountain meadow, locked on hers.

He'd taken off his hat, but by the way his dark,
unruly hair had been compressed, she doubted he
went without it very often.

His hand continued to hold hers in a warm grip,
his callused skin stimulating her senses and sending
a shimmy of heat up her arm and into her chest,
where it kicked her pulse up a notch.

"How do you do?" His voice, deep and gravelly, did
a real number on her, too, intriguing her as much as
his touch. Like his skin, it was weathered and sun
baked.

As he loosened his grip and released her, she
fought the impulse to clasp her empty hand to her
chest and study him like a mesmerized child on a
field trip to a Wild West museum.

Yet he hadn't *really* let go of her. The intensity in
his expression made it difficult for her to breathe, let
alone speak, and she wasn't at all sure why.

"Martin tells me that you speak Spanish," Mr.
Callaghan said.

She cleared the cobwebs from her throat. "Yes, I do. Fluently."

He nodded, as though she'd passed some kind of hurdle. And it pleased her that she had. Working with one of the firm's top clients gave her a bit of a professional rush.

Or was it the man himself?

There was something about Clay Callaghan that appealed to her, interested her. His cowboy demeanor, she supposed. The way he stood when a lady entered the room. The fact that he didn't carry his wealth and success the way another man might.

He had fifteen or twenty years on her, she suspected. But it didn't seem to matter at all—professionally, speaking, of course.

Martin pushed his chair back from his cherry wood desk, placed his elbows on the armrests and steepled his fingers. "Nearly a year ago, while participating in a semester abroad program in Guadalajara, Trevor, Clay's only child, was killed in a car accident."

"I'm sorry," she said, her gaze lighting on the brooding client and recognizing it was grief that clouded his expression.

Mr. Callaghan didn't respond, allowing Martin to continue.

"A couple of hours ago, he received word that Trevor fathered a child while in Mexico. He needs to fly out this afternoon and pick up his orphaned granddaughter. He's going to need an attorney, as well as an interpreter, to go with him."

She nodded.

Uh-oh. He'd also just asked if she spoke Spanish. Were they suggesting that she...?

Think fast, she prodded herself.

"How long will it take for you to pack?" Martin asked her.

Dani struggled to keep her reaction casual and like that of any other twenty-five-year-old, unmarried professional who didn't have any pressing family obligations to consider.

She could think of a multitude of reasons why Martin should ask another attorney to make the trip. First of all, there was the issue of her anxiety—God, she hated to fly. Just the thought of taking off in a plane and heading to Mexico scared the liver out of her. Second, she couldn't just up and leave the kids. She'd need to find a competent sitter, which wouldn't be easy. Then there was the fact that she'd volunteered to take Marcos and Delia to a movie tonight. Even sitting through a whacky cartoon this evening, followed by *Revenge of the Zombies,* was more appealing than going on a business trip to Mexico.

She opened her mouth to object, then realized refusing to go might jeopardize her career.

Martin cleared his throat in a way that made her realize he wasn't pleased with her lack of enthusiasm. "Is there a problem with you leaving this afternoon, Daniela?"

Maybe her job didn't hang in the balance, but her reputation as a career-minded employee did. So she swallowed her reluctance, as well as her anxiety about flying. "No, there isn't a problem. But I'll need a little time to…uh…ensure things are taken care of in my absence."

"How much time?" the Marlboro Man asked. "I'd like to leave as soon as possible."

"An hour or two," she said, thinking it wasn't enough. "But I'll do my best to hurry."

"Then what are you waiting for?" Martin asked. "Clay's pilot is having the plane fueled right now and working on a flight plan."

"If you'll give me your address," Mr. Callaghan said, "I'll pick you up. Or better yet, why don't I follow you home? We can leave from there."

Follow her home? To *her* house? The one with the kite stuck in the tree out front? The one with the bent screen in the living room window, where Sara had climbed in after Marcos had locked her out? The house with the lawn that needed to be mowed? The one that at this very moment held a trio of squabbling children?

Over the past few months, she'd done her best to make sure her colleagues and clients thought of her as the girl wonder, not The Old Woman Who Lived in the Shoe. She'd be darned if she'd sacrifice her image now.

"Actually," she said to the wealthy cowboy who looked as though he didn't take no for an answer, "I'd much rather meet you here at the office."

"I'm already packed," he said, "so I'll be waiting."

Great. More pressure.

She'd be perspiring like a foundry worker in mid-July by the time she returned.

But if she didn't get out of here and back in less than two hours, her carefully orchestrated career was in serious trouble.

Dani grumbled between cell phone calls, but by the time she'd arrived home, she'd managed to find someone to look after the kids while she was gone. And she'd also finagled a trip to Burgerland and a movie for Marcos and Delia.

Sofia Fuentes, the seventy-year-old widow who lived down the street, agreed to stay at the house and babysit for a day or two, but she had a weekend trip planned with her bridge group and was leaving on Friday morning.

Dani had no idea how long she'd be gone, but she'd have her cell phone, charger and address book in case she had to make alternate arrangements. The trip shouldn't take more than a day or so—unless they were waylaid with paperwork in Guadalajara.

The first thing she did when she walked through the front door was snatch the newspaper and scan the movie listings, choosing one that the younger children and Mrs. Fuentes would appreciate. Then, with Delia hot on her heels, she rushed to her bedroom to pack.

She didn't have a clue as to what the weather was like in Guadalajara, so she took twice as many clothes as she'd need. As she carefully placed her things in the old suitcase that had been her father's, she realized it was pretty battered and not in the style of a career-minded professional. But that was too bad. She was doing the best she could, under the circumstances.

"How come you have to go away for the whole night?" Delia asked, as she peered into Dani's room. "Who's going to read me the next chapter of *Charlotte's Web* when I go to bed?"

"I'm sure Mrs. Fuentes will read it to you," Dani said.

Marcos, who stood in the doorway, asked, "Will you take me to see *Revenge of the Zombies* when you get home?"

Dani wanted to say no, but she felt terrible about leaving like this. Guilt was an amazing thing, wasn't it? Especially when she suspected Marcos was using it to his advantage. But there wasn't much she could do about that now.

"What's the zombie movie rated?" she asked, as she took a quick inventory of her cosmetic bag, then packed it in the suitcase.

"It's PG-13, but not because anyone gets naked or because they say bad words. It's not even violent, because the Zombies have green blood and even a little kid knows that's fake."

Dani wasn't in the mood to debate the fact that the Motion Picture Association had rated it PG-13 for some reason. Or that a movie can be violent in spite of the color of a victim's blood and guts. "Okay, you and I can give it a try on Saturday. But if I decide it's inappropriate for a boy your age, we'll have to leave in the middle of it."

"You won't think that. I know 'cause my friends have all seen it. There aren't even guns and knives, just lasers and that sort of thing."

Yeah. Right.

Dani glanced at the clock on the bureau. Shoot. An hour and twenty minutes had already passed, and it would take fifteen minutes to get back to the office—unless she hit traffic.

The fact that Mr. Callaghan was waiting for her made her move faster, causing her hands to shake as she snapped the suitcase lid into place.

Then she kissed the kids goodbye, promising them treats if Mrs. Fuentes gave her a good report.

An hour and forty-two minutes after leaving the building, Dani returned with her suitcase in hand. She could feel the moisture building under her arms and along her scalp. But she mustered a smile and tried her best to act as though the errands she'd run had been similar to those of any single, twenty-five-year-old woman.

As she entered the reception area, Mr. Callaghan, who'd been waiting near the door, stood. The walls of the room seemed to close in on them, and she got a lungful of his musky, leathery scent.

"Ready?" The question slid over her like the whisper of a breeze on a sultry Houston night. Her heart, which was already pumping at a pretty good pace, began to beat erratically, which didn't make a bit of sense. She'd never been attracted to the cowboy type before. Or to a man who was nearly old enough to be her father.

Clay Callaghan was *so* not her type.

If she were in the market for romance—and God knows she wasn't—she would look for a successful young professional. Another attorney, maybe. Someone well-read, witty. Polished. Not a self-made man who couldn't kick his cowboy roots and might be twenty years her senior.

But tell that to the suddenly active hormones she'd kept under lock and key for the past couple of years.

She smiled, hoping it hid the fact that she might appear to be ready, but she wasn't eager to travel on a small plane with an important client, a man she didn't know very well, a rugged outdoorsman she was oddly attracted to.

"Yes," she lied. "Let's go."

* * *

As Clay took the suitcase from the pretty Latina's hand, his fingers brushed against hers. Their eyes locked, and something sparked between them. Something he had no business contemplating, especially since it seemed to fluster the hell out of her.

Damn, she was young. And pretty. She wore her glistening black hair swept up in a professional twist, although a few strands had escaped. It had been neatly coiffed before, but not so anymore. He suspected her rush to get packed, run a few errands and race back to the office had rumpled her.

That was okay with him. He wasn't attracted to women who wore business suits or who had to powder their noses and reapply lipstick all day long.

Not that he was on the prowl these days. Or that he had time to do anything more right now than fly to Guadalajara, pick up the baby and head home. They'd be gone one night and a day, best he could figure.

Of course, that was assuming the child was Trevor's. But until he got her home and ran a DNA test, he wouldn't know for sure.

And if she wasn't his flesh and blood?

Then he'd talk to his foreman, "Hawk" Hawkins, whose brother and sister-in-law had been trying to conceive for years and were talking adoption.

Either way, he'd face that road when he came to it. Clay might have made a lot of mistakes with his son over the years, but he wouldn't fail his granddaughter.

He opened the office door for Daniela, then followed her out into the hall.

She fingered the side of her hair, just now realizing she was falling apart, and a grin tugged at his lips. For an attorney who was supposed to be bright and capable, she seemed a little ill-at-ease to him.

She'd just passed the bar, he'd been told. And had a slew of recommendations from her professors at law school, not to mention she was second in her class.

That was impressive, he supposed, assuming someone was big on academics, which he wasn't. The most valuable lessons were learned in the real world. That's why going to college had never crossed Clay's mind. Instead he'd prided himself on his ranching skills, his common sense and an innate head for business. He'd done all right for himself. Hell, he had more money than he knew what to do with.

At the elevator, Daniela punched the down button, then glanced up at him and smiled. She had to be closer to twenty than thirty, if you asked him. Of course, it might just be her size. She only stood a little over five feet tall and was just a slip of a thing.

The elevator buzzed, and when the door opened, they stepped inside.

"So tell me about your granddaughter," she asked.

"There's not much to tell. I've never seen her before."

"How old is she?"

He shrugged. "I forgot to ask."

She cocked her head, perplexed, he supposed. But he didn't see what the kid's age had to do with anything, other than prove that it was possible Trevor had fathered her.

"The baby has to be less than a year old," he said, "but more than two months."

As they continued their descent to the ground floor, the scent of her perfume swirled in the elevator. It was something soft and powdery. Peaches and cream, he guessed.

"Are you sure the child is your son's?" she asked.

"Nope." But the fact that it might be was reason enough to go to Mexico and bring her home.

"There are blood tests that can prove paternity," she said.

He nodded. "Yeah. I know that." He'd have the test run after he got back in the States. "But let's take this one step at a time."

"And that first step would be…?"

"Getting that baby home."

When they reached the ground floor, the elevator opened and they entered the spacious lobby.

Clay stepped ahead, then opened the smoky-glass double doors and escorted her outside and down the walkway to the parking lot. "My truck is in the second row. To the left."

When they reached the stall where he'd parked

his black, dual-wheeled Chevy pickup, he pulled the keys out of his pocket and clicked the lock. He tossed her suitcase in the bed of the truck and opened the passenger door. Then he removed his duffle bag and waited for her to climb inside.

She bit down on her bottom lip, as she perused the oversize tires that made the cab sit higher than usual. He couldn't help but grin. She was going to have a hell of a time climbing into the seat with that tight skirt. An ornery part of him thought he'd stick around and watch the struggle. She placed a hand on the door, then lifted her foot and placed it on the running board.

Pretty legs.

"Need some help?" he asked.

"No, I can manage."

Rather than gawk, which he had half a notion to do, he tossed his bag in the back of the truck. As she continued to pull herself into the Chevy, the fabric of her skirt pulled tight against her rounded hips. She might be petite, but she was womanly. And damn near perfectly shaped.

She slid into the seat, then glanced around the cab. "Where are the baby's things?"

The baby's things? Hell, he hadn't given that any thought. All he'd wanted to do was talk to his attorney, fly to Mexico, get the kid and head home.

She crossed her arms, causing her breasts to strain against the fabric of her blouse. "Don't tell me you don't have anything packed for an infant?"

Okay, he wouldn't tell her that. But he didn't have squat for the kid. In fact, he wasn't prepared to take on a baby at all, and in his rush to get to Mexico, he hadn't given supplies any thought. Nor had he given much thought to what he'd do with the kid, once he got her home.

"I don't know much about babies or their needs. Hell, I never even held my son until he was close to two."

"Well then, like you said, we'll need to take this one step at a time. I suggest you stop by Spend-Mart. It's just down the street and ought to have everything you need."

"I hope you have a few suggestions. I don't have a clue what to get."

"Believe it or not, I have a pretty good idea. But it won't be cheap."

Neither was the trip to Mexico. But money was the last thing Clay had considered. Not when he was still carrying a ton of grief over Trevor's death.

The pastor who'd spoken at the memorial had told Clay it would take time. But so far the weight on his chest hadn't eased up a bit.

Minutes later Clay and Daniela entered the crowded department store.

"Get a shopping cart," she told him, taking the lead. For some fool reason, Clay, who never was one to follow orders, complied.

In no time at all, she had the cart filled with disposable diapers, wipes, ointments, lotions, pacifiers. Next, she threw in bottles, formula—both ready-made in the can and powdered in packets—plus a couple of jugs of water. Then she zeroed in on receiving blankets, pajamas, undershirts and clothes.

"You already have one of those," he said, nodding to the pink and white PJs. "But in purple."

"We don't know what size she wears, so we'll keep the receipt and return whatever doesn't fit."

Clay merely nodded his head as he followed the pretty, dark-haired attorney through the baby section.

For a single woman, she sure was adept at knowing what things he was going to need. What an intriguing contradiction she was. On the outside, she seemed every bit as professional and competent as Martin Phillips had insisted she was. But there was obviously a maternal and domestic side to her, as well.

"This ought to get us started," she said. "You can go shopping again, after you get her home."

"Maybe you can do that for me," he said.

She arched a brow. "My fees are $250 an hour. I'm sure you can find someone better qualified and cheaper."

"But maybe not someone who knows as much about kids as you do."

He meant it as a joke, as a way of telling her he didn't give a damn about the cost. But she stiffened for a moment, then seemed to shrug it off.

"I did a lot of babysitting in the past," she explained.

"Lucky me."

As they headed for the checkout lines, he couldn't help but watch her. She seemed to be counting each item she'd chosen, taking inventory. Making sure they had all they needed.

So she'd spent her early years babysitting. Maybe her beginnings had been as humble as his.

She was interesting. Intriguing.

And attractive.

Not that he'd ever chase after a woman who would have been more his son's type. And one who was definitely more his son's age.

Chapter Two

Thirty minutes later Clay and Daniela arrived at Hobby Airport in Houston, where Roger Tolliver, Clay's pilot, had already filed a flight plan and was waiting to take off. Roger, a retired air force captain with thousands of hours of experience, was doing his final check of the twin-engine King Air, which Clay had purchased from the factory last year.

After parking his truck and unloading their luggage and purchases, Clay removed the baby's car seat from the box so it would fit in the plane better. Then he juggled it and the heavier items, along with a briefcase, a black canvas gym bag that carried a change of clothing and his shaving gear.

"It's this way," Clay told Daniela, who carried her purse, a small brown suitcase and several blue plastic shopping bags, as he headed toward the plane.

The competent young attorney, who'd been leading the way through Spend-Mart and racking up a significant charge on Clay's American Express, was now taking up the rear. Clay had a feeling it wasn't the load she was carrying that caused her to lag behind.

He glanced over his shoulder and, shouting over the noise of a red-and-white Cessna that had just landed, asked, "What's the matter?"

"Nothing." She carefully eyed his plane, as well as the salt-and-pepper-haired pilot.

"Don't tell me you're skittish about flying," he said.

"All right. I won't."

Great. His traveling companion was a nervous wreck. Maybe, if she felt more confident about the man in charge of the plane, she'd relax.

When they reached the King Air, Clay greeted the pilot. "Roger Tolliver, this is my attorney, Daniela de la Cruz."

"Pleased to meet you, ma'am." The older man took the bags from her hands.

"As you can see," Clay told Roger, "we've got quite a few things to take along. Daniela reminded me that we'd need supplies for the baby, so we bought out the infant department at Spend-Mart."

"I had a couple kids of my own, so I know how much paraphernalia is needed." Roger nodded toward the steps that would make it easy to board the plane. "Why don't you make yourselves comfortable. I'll pack this stuff."

Before long, the hatch was secured, and they were belted in their seats. As they taxied to the runway, Clay couldn't help but glance at the woman beside him, her face pale and her eyes closed. White-knuckled fingers clutched the armrests of her seat. She sat as still and graceful as a swan ice sculpture on a fancy buffet table. The only sign of movement was near her collarbone, where the beat of her heart pulsed at her throat.

Damn. She really *was* nervous.

"Daniela," Clay said over the drone of the engine, thinking he'd make light of it, tease her a bit to get her mind on something else. But when she opened her eyes, her gaze pierced his chest, striking something soft and vulnerable inside. Without warning, the joke slipped away, and compassion—rare that it was—took its place. "Hey. Don't worry. Roger was flying before you were even born. He's got a slew of commendations from the air force. He'll get us to Mexico and back before dinnertime tomorrow."

"That's nice to know." She offered him a shy smile, then slid back into her frozen, sculptured pose.

According to Martin, the senior partner in the

firm and Daniela's boss, she was a bright, capable attorney. But she was clearly not a happy flyer.

Damn. This was going to be a hell of a long trip if she didn't kick back a little and relax.

Moments later the plane took off, heading for Guadalajara. Once they were airborne, Clay offered her a drink. "It ought to take the edge off your nervousness."

"I'm not big on alcohol," she said.

"How about a screwdriver?" he pressed. "Orange juice with just enough vodka to relax you?"

She pondered the idea momentarily. "All right. Maybe I should."

He got up and made his way to the rear of the plane—just a couple of steps, actually—and fixed her a drink from an ice chest Roger had prepared. He poured himself a scotch and water, too, then returned to his seat. "It's a pretty day. Take a look out the window."

She managed a quick peek, but didn't appear to be impressed.

"How long have you been working for Phillips, Crowley and Norman?" he asked.

"A little over a year."

He wondered what age that would make her. Pushing into the late twenties, probably. Hell, she wasn't much older than Trevor would have been. And he suspected she was probably the same studious, bookworm type as his son. College-educated folks usually were.

Clay and his son hadn't had a damn thing in com-mon—other than a love of flying the King Air and the Bonanza they'd owned before that. And though there'd been a bond of sorts, the two of them had butted heads more times than not.

Maybe if Clay's old man had stuck around long enough to be a father to him, it might have helped Clay know how to deal with his own son. But Glen Callaghan had been a drifter. Clay's only other role model had been Rex Billings, a gruff and crusty cat-tleman who used to hang out at The Hoedown, a seedy bar on the outskirts of Houston where Clay's mom worked as a waitress. When his mom was di-agnosed with terminal cancer, the old cowboy took her and Clay in, letting them live at his place.

Never having a family of his own, Rex hadn't quite known what to do with a ten-year-old boy, but he'd given it his best shot, teaching Clay how to be tough, how to be a man. There was never any doubt that Rex had come to love Clay, even though the words had never been said. And when Rex died, he left the Rocking B Ranch and everything he owned to the young man who'd become a son to him.

Clay had done his best to turn the cattle ranch into a multimillion dollar venture. And over the past twenty years, that's exactly what he'd done. He'd become a hell of a businessman. But in the long run, he'd been a crappy dad.

He'd tried his damnedest to teach Trevor the

things a boy ought to know, the things Rex had taught Clay: to be tough; to work hard; to suck it up without grumbling.

Trevor used to complain that Clay never had time for him. But hell, if the kid had gotten his nose out of those books he carried around and quit carping about his allergy to alfalfa, they might have gotten along as well as Rex and Clay had.

But that didn't mean Clay hadn't tried to reach out to the kid in his own way. He'd suggested a fishing trip when Trevor turned sixteen, but that idea had gone over like a sack of rotten potatoes. He'd also asked Trevor to accompany him to an auction, thinking they could hang out a few days afterward. But for some reason, you'd think Clay had suggested they go to the dentist for a root canal.

Clay wasn't sure what the boy had expected from him. But instead of having the kind of relationship either of them might have liked, they merely passed each other in the hall.

Of course, he'd meant to remedy that when Trevor got a little older—and a little wiser—hoping that after his son graduated from college, they'd find some common ground. He'd kept telling himself that things would be better between them—one of these days.

But one of these days came and went.

Clay tried to tell himself he hadn't failed completely. He'd tried to make up for things in other ways, like buying Trevor a state-of-the-art computer system, paying for out-of-state tuition and allowing him to go on that international study abroad program that landed him in Guadalajara, where he died.

And there it went again. Full circle.

Thoughts of Trevor led to thoughts of his short-comings as a father and the load of guilt he carried for not doing something about it—whatever that might have been—when he'd had the chance. He did the best he could to shove the feelings aside, as Rex had taught him, forcing them to the dark pit in his chest.

What was done was done.

Clay may have failed Trevor, but he wasn't going to let his granddaughter down—assuming the baby was a Callaghan. So he looked out the window, focused his gaze straight ahead. Shoved those feelings down deep, where they belonged.

Thirty minutes or more into the flight, Daniela had managed to finish her vodka-laced juice and had seemed to relax a bit—until they hit an air pocket. Then she paled.

"Sorry about that." Roger glanced over his shoulder and caught Clay's eye. "Better fasten your seat belts, folks. It's going to be bumpy for a while."

The pilot nodded toward the windshield at the dark gray sky ahead. Roger planned to fly around the storm. And he'd warned Clay earlier that it would be a bumpy flight, although there was no reason to suggest they would be taking any unnecessary chances. Clay was, however, determined to get the baby out of Mexico and back to the States as quickly as he could, so he would have agreed to any risk Roger was willing to make. Still, he hated seeing Daniela so uneasy.

Under normal circumstances, with any other attorney, he would have been annoyed. But there was something about Daniela that made her different. And it wasn't just her gender and her youthful beauty.

Okay, maybe it was.

Clay had never been one to chase after younger women. He preferred someone with maturity, someone who wasn't interested in settling down.

Hell, he'd never even married his son's mother. He and Sally had met at the feed lot and had a brief but heated affair. There hadn't been much emotion involved. Of course, there never was on Clay's part, and he always managed to find a lover with the same no-strings philosophy. Sally hadn't seen any reason to get married, either, which was a relief.

As the plane hit another rough spot, he stole a glance at his traveling companion. Distress clouded her expression, the contradiction of competent attorney and frightened passenger intriguing him. Hell, he couldn't sit idly by and watch her come apart at the seams—no matter how much he enjoyed looking at her.

"It shouldn't be much longer," Roger said.

The plane bounced again, causing Daniela to nearly drop her drink.

"Finish it," Clay told her, and she quickly obliged. He wondered if she assumed his order had been due to safety reasons, but it didn't matter. He was just hoping she'd consume enough alcohol to feel more at ease. So far, it didn't seem to be working.

The next time the plane dipped, she reached across the aisle and grabbed his hand, gripping him tightly.

Her touch, as well as her vulnerability, struck an unfamiliar chord in him, and he found himself stroking the top of her wrist with his thumb, comforting her much the way he would a skittish filly.

"That should be the worst of it," Roger announced.

Yet Daniela didn't let go.

Her hand was small, her nails unpolished and filed neatly, her skin soft. Yet her grip was strong.

Clay had half a notion to draw her close, to offer her more than a hand to hold.

Now where the hell had that wild-ass thought come from?

Clay had never been one to mess with the touchy-feely stuff. And the fact that he'd let down his guard and nearly done so, didn't sit well with him. So he did the only thing he could think of. He offered her another drink.

Interestingly enough, she agreed without much hesitation.

"A little turbulence is no big deal," Clay told her. "Really. Think of this as a car going along a bumpy road."

Yeah, right, Dani thought.

When it came to aerodynamics, that was probably true. But it felt as though there were only clouds holding them up, and the waters of the gulf below were waiting to swallow them whole. That is, unless they'd already crossed over the Mexican border, in which case…

Oh, for Pete's sake. Her fear of flying was as real as it was embarrassing.

She knew what Clay was doing. He was trying to make her feel better, and she appreciated his efforts.

"I don't suppose we have to let Martin know about this, do we?" She took a sip of her drink, expecting to scrunch her face at the taste of the vodka and force herself to swallow. But this second screwdriver tasted better and seemed to be going down a lot easier than the first.

"Let Martin know about what?" the rugged rancher asked as if he hadn't picked up on her distress.

"I had a bad experience a few years ago," she admitted. "We almost crashed. Once we got back on the ground, I swore I'd never get in a plane again, at least not a small one."

He took a swig of his scotch, then nodded at her glass. "Drink up. Then let's share battle stories."

"You had a frightening experience, too?" she asked.

"More than my share—on the land, air and sea. But I've always lived to tell about them."

She took another big swallow, then decided to reveal her one-and-only adventure first. "When I was in college, some friends invited me to ski with them in Vail. Between them, they loaned me all the gear, and one of our classmates had a private plane and a brand-new pilot's license."

The memory alone was enough to bring on a shudder, but talking about it seemed to help, making her realize this trip wasn't anywhere near as awful. Not yet, anyway.

"College students on their way to a party and a spanking-new pilot," Clay said, sizing up her experience. "That sounds like a bad mix to me."

"We weren't going to a party," Dani corrected.

She'd always been too responsible for that, too diligent with her studies to play. But it had been winter break, and she'd always wanted to know what the fuss was about snow skiing.

"So what happened?" Clay sat back in his seat, his legs extended, a long, lean cowboy completely at ease. His calm demeanor was reassuring, his presence comforting. As were the two drinks he'd fixed her.

So she settled, somewhat, into her seat. "The sky darkened, and lightning bolts shot all around us. The thunder was incredibly loud, and the turbulence was terrifying. We bounced around like a splatter of water on a hot griddle, and after what seemed like forever, we finally landed in Denver."

"See?" he said, taking another drink, chunks of ice clinking against the glass. "You came out all right."

"Yes, but I also left my friends in Colorado, purchased a bus ticket and went home before the weekend got underway."

Without asking, Clay fixed them each another drink. Dani should have politely declined, but took it from him anyway. To be honest, the taste wasn't so bad anymore. And the intoxicating effect had numbed her nerves to a tolerable level. Of course, the plane was also traveling smoothly now—or relatively, she supposed.

By the time she'd downed her third drink, she decided Clay Callaghan was not only a handsome older man, but he was also the nicest guy she'd ever met. He was very quiet, a great listener.

Or maybe the alcohol had loosened her tongue. Either way, she found herself babbling about one thing or another. After she'd told him about how hard she'd worked to pass Chemistry 103, Clay paused a beat, considering her.

"So you were the studious sort." A slow grin

deepened the lines around his eyes—green, with flecks of gold that glimmered—and brought out an interesting pair of dimples. "I thought all college kids liked to party."

"Not me. I was practically born responsible. I *had* to be."

"Why?"

She shrugged. "My mom was a lot younger than my dad. I guess you could say she was flighty and irresponsible. When I was in kindergarten, she left us, so Dad and I had to fend for ourselves. Even as a five-year-old, I tried to do everything I could to make things easier for him. For us, actually."

"At the age of five? That's a mighty big chore for a little girl."

"It wasn't so bad. I helped with laundry and cooking. By the time I was ten, I could fix a hearty meal."

"So the attorney is a whiz in the kitchen, as well as the courtroom."

"If you like Mexican food."

"That's it?"

"Well, I can fix a pretty decent casserole, as long as I have a box and all the fixings." She tossed him a smile.

His lips quirked as though he found her entertaining, and it warmed her heart. It warmed her cheeks, too.

In fact, it was getting hot in here.

"Whew." She fanned herself with both hands.

Clay chuckled as though he wasn't at all bothered by the temperature or by her attempts to cool off. "Well, now that you're a high-priced attorney, you ought to be able to hire a chef."

"Yeah, right." She took off her jacket and laid it on an empty seat. Then she kicked off her shoes and rubbed her bare feet along the carpeting. "With three kids to raise and student loans to repay?"

"You've got three kids?" His voice rose an octave and a decibel level, bearing evidence of his surprise. As his gaze roamed over her, it seemed to peel away her clothes, as well as her facade.

But for some reason she didn't care. In fact, she felt compelled to confide in him. "I'm not their birth mother, if that's what you think. My dad remarried when I was ten. And my stepmom wanted a family of her own. So pretty soon the babies started coming, and I helped out with them, too."

"You sure took on a lot of responsibility in your family." His voice returned to normal, that deep, graveled drawl that seemed to suit him so well. A pleasurable sound a woman could get used to. "When did you manage to find time to study?"

"In the late evenings, when the house was quiet." She smiled. "But it wasn't that bad. Academics came easy for me and I did very well in high school. College, too. I even received a partial scholarship to Rice University."

"I bet your family was proud."

"They were. My dad and stepmom were struggling financially, but they managed to supplement the scholarship. They only asked that I provide financial assistance for the younger children's college education."

"Sort of a pay it forward thing, huh?"

"Well, that was the idea."

The agreement they'd made had fostered her desire to excel first in school, then in her profession—and quickly. But she hadn't counted on the unexpected. "During my first year of law school, my stepmom died in a car accident, and I nearly dropped out. My younger brother and sisters needed me. And so did my dad."

"Obviously, you didn't quit."

"No. Somehow, I managed to make it through. Believe it or not, having a goal on which to focus made it easier to deal with the grief."

"No one understands that more than I do," Clay said. "You're a strong young woman, Daniela."

She leaned forward. "You think so?" Then she blew out a sigh, along with all the secrets she kept shoved into the bottom or her heart. "It's been a struggle sometimes. Especially after my dad died."

"That's too bad." His concern was touching, and the sound of his voice was growing on her moment by moment. It was nice. Rough yet soft. Sympathetic and supportive.

"Did your father pass away recently?" he asked.

"Yes, last year. He was fishing with some friends in the gulf and was killed in a freak boating accident."

"I'm sorry," he said again, the rugged, sexy drawl a balm.

"That's okay. I'm doing fine. Really." Yet tears welled in her eyes. She tried to blink them away, but they soon overflowed and slid down her cheeks. She swiped at them, struggling to keep up with the flow.

"Darn it. I don't understand why this is happening. I haven't cried in a long time and can't understand why I'm so weepy and emotional now." She sought his gaze, hoping he wouldn't hold her display of tears against her.

"Tell me about the kids," he said, as though maneuvering around the subject.

"They're a handful. Sara, my fourteen-year-old sister, constantly complains about having to help me keep an eye on the others. And Marcos, who is ten, never fails to let me know what a pain it is to be the only boy in a family full of girls. Little Delia, who truly is a sweetheart, cries at the drop of the hat."

"That's gotta be tough."

"It is. And I'm doing a poor job of it." Dani blew out a weary sigh. "I love them. I really do. But it's tough trying to support them, both emotionally and financially, by myself."

He didn't respond, but she sensed his understanding, his sympathy.

She reached across the aisle, placing her hand on his muscular forearm. "But don't feel sorry for me. I'm going to make a name for myself at Phillips, Crowley and Norman."

"I bet you will."

"Do you know what?"

He shook his head no.

"Martin and everyone else at the firm think I'm a single, career-minded woman with no other responsibilities but my job." So far she'd had them all fooled. But she feared her secret wouldn't last long.

"Don't be so hard on yourself," he said.

"I try not to be." But if truth be told, sometimes, late at night, when the kids finally went to bed and the house was quiet, seeds of resentment sprouted— when she let them. She was forced to admit to herself that the responsibility she'd inherited was overwhelming.

She opened her mouth to reveal that to Clay, as well, but for some reason, she clamped her jaw shut. Something told her she might have said too much already.

What all had she told him?

Clay glanced at his watch. "We ought to be getting pretty close to Guadalajara now."

Dani peered out the window. Oh, wow. It was really dark outside.

"How much longer will it be?" Clay asked Roger.

"See those lights ahead?" the pilot asked. "We'll be landing in about fifteen minutes. Are you planning to go to the church tonight?"

"No," Clay said. "From what I've been told, the road to the village isn't that easy to find in the daylight. So we'll get a couple of hotel rooms. Then we'll hire a driver to take us at the crack of dawn."

What a day this had proven to be, Dani thought. She'd flown to Mexico and was going to a hotel to spend the night with a client.

Well, not exactly *with* him…

She stole a glance at Clay, marveling at his chiseled features, the commanding way he had about him. Earlier today she'd thought him brooding and dark, but that was before she'd gotten to know him.

When she'd first met him, she decided that, for an older man, he was attractive, but now she was beginning to see that age had nothing to do with it.

Clay Callaghan was a hunk, plain and simple.

The plane veered a bit to the right, then the left, as it descended, and a wave of dizziness struck with a vengeance. Her tummy turned inside out.

Whew.

Thank goodness they wouldn't be going after the baby tonight.

Dani wasn't feeling very well, but if her luck held, no one would be the wiser.

Chapter Three

Upon arriving in Guadalajara and going through the port of entry check, Clay called the limousine service he'd lined up—a reputable company that had been recommended by a fellow cattleman who traveled regularly to Mexico on business. Then he, Roger and Daniela, who seemed to list to the side while walking, headed for the sleek, black luxury vehicle. The driver opened the door, and Clay held Daniela's arm—more in an effort to steady her than to be polite.

She wobbled, then stumbled. "Oops."

Clay reached for her, just as she lost her balance, and caught her, drawing her back against his chest.

His arms rested under the fullness of her breasts, his cheek against her hair. It had been a while since he'd held a woman close. Too long, he realized.

"Sorry." She glanced over her shoulder and tossed him a silly smile. "My foot slipped, and I almost fell. Thank you for not letting me."

"My pleasure."

"I'll bet it was," Roger said with a chuckle.

When they all got inside the car, the driver shut the door, then climbed behind the wheel and started the engine.

"Daniela," Clay said. "Tell him we're going to El Jardin. It's a hotel not far from here."

When she didn't respond, he turned and spotted her slouched in the seat, her eyes closed, her head tilted against the backrest.

"I think she passed out," Roger said.

Damn. Roger was right. Quite frankly, Clay found it amusing. But if she remembered in the morning, she'd probably be embarrassed.

"Vamos al hotel El Jardin," Clay told the driver.

"Sí, señor."

"Your Spanish sounds pretty good," Roger said.

"I can get by."

Roger nodded at Daniela. "So why the interpreter?"

"I wanted her along just in case we have any trouble with the law or the authorities. If that happens, we'll need someone with a better handle on the language than I have."

"You think so?"

Clay chuffed. "I know so. When I was nineteen, a buddy and I went to El Paso on business. We finished early, then decided to celebrate across the border in Juarez. We had a little too much to drink, I had a run-in with a couple of the locals and ended up in jail for nine scary days. And Rex, my…well, I guess you would call him my old man…spent quite a bundle to get me out. So I don't want to take any chances on this trip. We'll be in and out of here before you can count to *tres*."

"Do you want me to go with you to the church?" Roger asked.

"No. Wait for us here. Or we'll drop you off at the airport. Whatever you're comfortable with. Just have the plane fueled and ready to take off the moment we get back."

"You don't expect any problems?" Roger asked.

No. But there could be plenty. "I came prepared for almost everything." Clay studied the woman seated beside him. Better make that "slumped" beside him. "At least, I thought I did." A grin tugged at his lips. Damn, she was a cute drunk.

He'd only meant to see her relax, but he shouldn't have plied her with so many screwdrivers. He'd overdone it. His lovely young attorney was a real jabberbox when she drank too much.

He wondered how much of this day she'd remember in the morning. Not that he'd tell Martin about her family situation. Or her feelings of inadequacy with the kids. Even if Clay was prone to idle chatter—and he wasn't—who was he to cast stones at people with lousy parenting skills?

He'd raised Trevor for five years, and what did he have to show for it?

A couple of school pictures.

A roomful of books, clothes and things he'd yet to sort through.

An ache in his chest and a gut full of guilt.

Ten minutes later, the limousine pulled into the red-bougainvillea-lined drive of El Jardin, one of the nicest hotels in town. The white stucco building boasted Spanish tile floors, a hand-crafted stone fountain in the lobby and an Old-World charm that was hard to beat.

Roger sat in the car with Daniela, while Clay checked in. And after securing the keys to three separate rooms, he returned to the limo.

"*Venga por nosotros mañana,*" Clay told the driver, giving him instructions to return at the crack of dawn. "*A las seis.*"

"*Muy bien,*" the driver responded. "*Hasta mañana, señor.*"

As the bellman loaded their luggage and belongings, Clay studied the woman sleeping in the vehicle.

"How do you plan to get her to her room?" Roger asked.

"Throw her over my shoulder, I guess." Clay shot the pilot a conspiratorial grin.

"No kidding? Like a sack of grain?"

"Come on, Roger. I'll be a gentleman." Then Clay stooped and reached into the car. "Hey...Daniela. Wake up."

She mumbled something and tried to scoot forward, but her efforts weren't especially effective. With his help, she managed to climb from the car, then swayed on her feet.

Not again, Clay thought as he caught her. But this time he scooped her into his arms.

Her eyes, the color of melted caramel, locked on his, and she grinned. "You're stronger than I expected."

"Nah, not really. You're just a lightweight." He meant her alcohol-tolerance level as well as her size.

"Think so?" She slipped her arms around his neck. "I haven't been carried by anyone in a long time."

"Oh, no? Then it's my lucky day." He took her into the lobby and waited for Roger to summon the elevator.

He juggled his lovely load, while handing the keys to Roger. "Take these. I've got my hands full."

As the lighted numbers indicated the elevator was slowly coming down to the lobby level, Daniela nuzzled her head against Clay's cheek and whispered, "You smell good."

"Thanks." So did she.

He savored the faint, powdery scent of her body lotion, a peach blossom scent, and the silk of her hair.

As the elevator doors opened, they stepped inside.

"Which floor?" the pilot asked.

"Third and fourth."

Roger studied the keys, taking the one that was engraved with 406 and returned the others to Clay. "You two can take the rooms on the third floor. I think it's best if you stay close to her. She may need a babysitter tonight, and that's a better job for you."

"Why?"

"For one reason, it looks like you've already got her under control." Roger chuckled. "And for another, my wife would turn me every which way but loose if she thought I'd put a pretty, drunken woman to bed when I'm supposed to be working."

When the elevator made the first stop, Clay got out. "I'll get her settled and wait for the bellman to bring her things."

Roger nodded, a wry grin pulling at his lips. Then the doors closed, leaving Clay and Daniela alone in the hall.

"Where are you taking me?" she asked.

"To bed."

Her eyes fluttered, and her gaze met his. "Oh, no, that isn't a good idea. I don't think Martin would approve."

Clay chuckled. Martin was a straight shooter and would undoubtedly come unglued. Even if Clay would let himself succumb to that kind of temptation, he wouldn't take advantage of her inebriation. He liked his lovers to be willing participants.

"I wouldn't approve of it, either," he told her.

"Approve of what?"

That was the point. She wasn't in any condition to be truly willing.

When he reached room 312, he set her feet on the floor, then unlocked the door and let her inside.

She was walking now, without help. But she immediately kicked off her shoes and removed her jacket. Next she began to unbutton her blouse.

"Hang on there, Daniela."

"You keep calling me that, but now that we're friends, you should call me Dani."

"All right. But why don't you wait to get undressed until the bellman brings your bag up here?"

"Okay. Good idea." She plopped down on the bed. "Where are you going to sleep?"

"I have a room down the hall."

When a knock sounded at the door, Clay let the bellman in, pointed out which suitcase stayed and which things went to the other rooms. Then he gave the young man a generous tip.

If the bellman—Paco, according to the badge on his shirt—wondered where the baby was who went with all the stuff going to Clay's room, he didn't ask.

"Gracias," Paco said, giving a slight bow before leaving.

Clay ought to leave, too, but he wanted to make sure Daniela—Dani—was settled in for the night and safe. "I've got a wakeup call scheduled for five o'clock. Are you going to be okay with that?"

She nodded. "I'm an early bird."

"Yeah. A little mockingbird." When she scrunched her face, obviously a bit perplexed, he chuckled. "You're a real jabberbox, Dani."

She titled her head. "I am? Do you mean that in a bad way?"

"No," he said. "Why don't you go into the bathroom and get ready for bed. I'll turn down the covers for you, okay?"

She slid him a grin. "Thanks, Clay. You're really a nice guy. A true gentleman."

Oh, yeah? Well he didn't feel so nice. Or even remotely like a gentleman.

"Thank you so much," she said.

For what? Taking her away from kids who probably needed her? Putting her on a plane when she was afraid of flying? Plying her full of alcohol, just to keep her from becoming troublesome?

Or for trying to make amends by seeing her safely to her room and tucking her into bed?

"You don't need to thank me."

"Yes I do. You've been so understanding and you tried so hard to get my mind off the flight." She got off the bed and started toward him, lifting her arms to offer him a hug.

She probably wouldn't feel so thankful in the morning.

As she approached, he was a bit stymied about what he ought to do. Go with the flow, he supposed. Why add to her embarrassment? But the closer she got and the more pronounced the scent of peach blossoms, the less noble he felt.

He tried to tell himself that it was no big deal. That people offered friendly hugs every day. He didn't, of course, but others did. So he didn't make a fuss about it.

Yet the moment she slipped her arms around him, his pulse kicked up a notch, his hormones went on alert and any thoughts of nobility or appreciation slipped by the wayside.

She pressed her soft breasts against his chest, and a jagged bolt of heat shot through his veins. Damn. There was nothing friendly going on with this embrace.

He reminded himself that she'd called him a gentleman. And as he'd told Roger, that's exactly what he planned to be…until something exploded between them. Something loaded with sexual arousal.

She seemed perplexed by it momentarily, then went on tiptoe and drew his mouth to hers.

At the moment of contact, the nice guy inside of him was toast, and a rebel took his place.

Her lips parted, and she whimpered softly, leaning into him in a move so natural that it unleashed a powerful surge of desire. As the kiss deepened, becoming hot and demanding, every possible reason why he shouldn't be doing this— and there were a slew of them—dissipated in the stuffy air of the hotel room and set off sparks like a Fourth of July night.

His hands roamed over her back, her hips, and he pulled her flush against him. He didn't care that this was a business arrangement. Or that she was young enough to be his daughter. He didn't care that he was on a mission to find Trevor's baby and get out of Mexico as soon as he could. All he wanted to do was steal a taste of the beautiful young woman in his arms—the woman who thought he was a great guy and a good listener. The woman who would surely learn soon enough that he was neither.

A surge of guilt, an ever-present reality since Trevor's death, reared its head.

He'd be damned if he could allow this to go any further. Not unless she was stone-cold sober.

He tore his lips from hers, his blood pumping, his breath ragged. "I think we'd better call this a night and pretend it didn't happen."

She swayed on her feet, reminding him he'd made the right decision. When they stepped apart, a flush on her neck declared her arousal had been every bit as powerful as his own.

"I, uh…" A large hank of hair had slipped out of her clip, and she looked as though she'd been ravished. Her eyes, heavy with arousal, peered at him. "Wow, Clay."

Wow was right.

He had no idea she would pack a kiss like that.

"I shouldn't have let you do that," she said.

He opened his mouth to object, to tell her she'd made the first move, but what good would that do them now? He'd been an eager participant. Besides, he was the only one with a grasp on reason.

She placed her fingertips against her lips, and her eyes widened, as though suddenly sobered by reality. The red tint on her cheeks revealed embarrassment. "Martin will—"

"It was no big deal," he insisted. "And it'll be our secret. No one will ever find out."

She nodded. "But he'll—"

"He'll never know." Clay raked a hand through his hair. "Listen, Dani. I told you, I've requested a five-o'clock wake up call. We're leaving at six. Do you need more time than that?"

She shook her head. "No, I'll be ready."

"Good." Then he turned and left her room.

Clay had no intention of allowing anything like that to happen again.

Yet the memory of her sweet kiss and an aching erection followed him to his room and threatened to keep him awake until the front desk called at five.

* * *

The next morning the telephone rang, and Dani woke with a start. She grabbed the receiver from the bedside table, and a voice announced in broken English that it was five o'clock.

As she sat up in bed, her head pounded, and she sighed. All she needed was a headache this morning. Fortunately, she'd packed a bottle of water in her bag, as well as aspirin.

She couldn't remember much about last night. Or even yesterday. Maybe that was just as well. But whispers of a memory here and there, as well as bits of dialogue, plagued her while she showered and dressed.

An uneasiness continued to hover over her as she fixed her hair, applied a swipe of lipstick and brushed on a light coat of mascara.

Think, she told herself. What happened yesterday?

She remembered panicking on the flight. And drinking too much. Had she said something she would be sorry for? Done something she might regret?

She studied her face in the mirror, looking beyond the pale, hung-over image. As a clear memory surfaced, she fingered her lips. She'd kissed him, long and deep. Clay Callaghan. One of the firm's top clients.

And a darn good kisser.

Her cheeks heated with embarrassment. All she'd meant to do was prove herself as a competent attorney. What had she done instead? She'd completely lost her head and swapped tongues with a client. Was that any way to prove her professional ability?

What else had happened last night?

Why couldn't she remember it all? Why just scraps of conversation?

I'm an early bird.

Yeah. A mockingbird.

...a little jabberbox...

Oh, God. What in the world had she told him? How would she ever face him? Or better yet, what was she going to do if Martin got wind of it?

She'd better get a handle on this, come up with a spin.

A handle on *what?* she asked herself. She couldn't even remember anything to be embarrassed about.

Maybe it was best if she pretended nothing had happened. If something was said, if some indiscretion cropped up, she'd claim no knowledge of it.

It was the only feasible option.

The phone rang again, and she answered. "Hello?"

"Are you up?" a familiar, sexy voice asked.

"Yes."

"You feeling okay?"

"Of course." Had he known how tipsy she'd been yesterday?

There was no response, which she appreciated. Or should she actually be more concerned?

Shaking off her uneasiness and trying to claim some control over the situation, she asked, "Where are the baby things?"

"I have them in my room."

Thank goodness. "You're bringing them down to the lobby, right? We'll need them if we decide to bring the baby back to the hotel."

"I know." He paused again, then asked, "How did you sleep?"

"Fine." She cleared her throat. "In fact, never better. How about you?"

"I didn't sleep worth a damn."

Did she dare ask why? Nope. Not on her life. "That's too bad."

Another bout of silence, this one longer than the last. She hoped it was enough time to allow the memories to gel—and one did.

The touch of his lips, the stimulating scratch of his bristled jaw. The scent of his musky, mountain-fresh cologne.

"Well, we'd better head downstairs," he said. "The limousine is probably waiting."

"We're taking a limo?" she asked.

"The same one we used last night."

They went somewhere in a limo? If so, she'd better fake it. "I just wondered."

"We're burning daylight so, if you're ready, let's go, Dani."

Dani.

He'd called her the name reserved for family and friends. The name her colleagues and clients never used. But there was no time to consider why.

"I'll be right down," she said.

When the line disconnected, she grumbled under her breath, cursing the alcohol and swearing to never drink again.

Minutes later, Dani and Clay climbed into a black limousine. The driver smiled at her as if he knew something she didn't, and the fact that he might didn't sit well with her at all.

"Where's Roger?" she asked.

"He's sleeping in."

The lid of the trunk popped open in back, and a bellman loaded their luggage.

"I need that baby stuff in here," she said. "I want to have it handy. There's a diaper bag I need to pack."

Clay got out and had the bellman pull the items from the trunk and pile them into the back of the car. Then they took off.

"Where are we headed?" she asked, trying to focus on the future, rather than the past twenty-four hours.

"To Rio Seco. It's a small village about thirty kilometers outside of town."

"Do you know who has the baby?"

"Father Luis Fernando. He's the priest of a small parish."

When Clay didn't offer any more information, she decided it was better not to ask. Maybe, once they got to Rio Seco and decided what Clay wanted to do about the baby, she'd be able to prove herself again. She'd help him get the paperwork in order and face the legalities of transporting the baby back to the States.

Then maybe he'd forget about everything else that had happened yesterday. She certainly was going to do her best to put it all behind her—her nervousness on the plane, her drinking—yet something told her she'd be hard-pressed to forget the kiss they'd shared.

A kiss that would haunt her in more ways than one.

Chapter Four

On the drive to Rio Seco, Dani focused on packing the diaper bag and tried her best to ignore the man beside her. Clay, who stared out the window at the scenery, didn't seem to be bothered by the silence. Perhaps he'd come to the same conclusion that she had. It was best to forget whatever had happened yesterday.

Moments later he turned his attention to her, watching as she placed disposable diapers and wipes in the bag with a Winnie the Pooh print. She pulled out a can from the case of ready-made formula. "This stuff is more expensive than the powder and bulkier to transport, but I was worried about the water supply."

"The baby has already been drinking the water," he said.

She hadn't thought of that. "Still, maybe we should have purchased another case of the formula."

"Don't worry about it. We won't be here very long."

That might not be true. The process could be more involved than he expected, which was why she'd been so concerned about leaving the kids with a sitter.

From what Dani had gathered, the wealthy rancher was used to having things go his way, but there were certain steps that needed to be taken, so he was going to have to adjust and be patient.

"Leaving here with her isn't the problem," she said. "It's landing in Houston and dealing with Customs and Border Protection. That baby is a Mexican citizen."

"Sometimes money can speed things up."

Dani bristled. "Don't tell me that. I won't be a part of anything illegal."

"I wouldn't ask you to." He didn't explain, and she let it drop.

Thirty minutes later they arrived in Rio Seco, a small town where the church was located. From outward appearances—the old vehicles, the weathered structures—it was easy to see the community was poor, but the buildings were clean.

Children playing with a ball and stick in the dirt

road froze in awe at the sight of the limousine, then trotted along after the slow-moving vehicle until it pulled in front of a quaint but rustic church made of adobe and rough-hewn beams.

"Come on," Clay said. "Let's go find the padre."

He didn't wait for the driver to open the door for them. And once he was outside the vehicle, he reached for Dani's hand and helped her exit. Then they strode into the church.

A middle-aged woman wearing a rosary and a white lace veil on her head was walking out as they entered.

"¿Dónde está el Padre?" Dani asked her.

"En su oficina." The woman pointed to a door to the left of the candlelit altar.

Their shoes clicked upon the scarred tile floor as they made their way to the church office.

"The padre speaks English," Clay said, as he knocked.

Moments later an old priest answered, and upon seeing Clay, recognition dawned on his wrinkled face. He brightened. "Señor Callaghan. You are the man who stood beside your son in the photograph with the airplane, no?"

Clay nodded.

The short, stocky man looked at Dani and grinned. "Señora Callaghan?"

"No," Clay corrected quickly. "This is my attorney, Daniela de la Cruz."

The old priest reached out a gnarled hand and greeted Dani with a smile. "It is nice to meet you."

"Mucho gusto," she told him.

"Where is the baby?" Clay asked, clearly focused on his task.

"Come this way." The priest guided them out a side door, through a colorful rose garden someone had lovingly tended, along a walkway flanked by orange and yellow marigolds and toward one of two buildings in back. Both could use a new coat of white paint, but the grounds were clean and neat. Wooden steps led to the front door of a white stucco building. Not exactly a house, Dani decided, but she suspected it was the priest's living quarters.

Luis Fernando wiped his feet on a woven mat, then led them into a small sitting room, where various pieces of religious artwork adorned white plastered walls. A bookshelf made of dark wood displayed a respectable library.

An elderly nun wearing a black habit sat at a desk near the window. She glanced up from her work when they entered and offered a smile.

"Maria Teresa," the priest said, as he began the introductions. Then, in Spanish, he asked her to please get the baby.

She nodded respectfully, then left the room.

"As I explained when we talked on the telephone," the padre told Clay, "Catalina, the baby's mother, died the day after her birth, leaving her with

Manuela Vargas, a woman from our village. Some call Manuela a witch, others say she is crazy. I don't agree with either side. She is just a bitter old woman who has her own interpretation of scripture."

"Why was Catalina staying with her?" Clay asked.

"Catalina was the daughter of Manuela's nephew, I believe. I'm not sure of the exact relationship, but there is a connection." He swept an arm toward the small sofa and several wooden chairs. "Please have a seat."

Dani and Clay complied.

"Will Catalina's family agree to an adoption?" Dani asked.

"They disowned their daughter," the padre said. "And Manuela believes God punished Catalina for her sins by allowing her to die. I'm afraid she believes the baby will suffer the same fate."

Dani cringed at the darkness of a belief like that.

The priest walked to the desk where the nun had been sitting, pulled open a drawer, withdrew a small black box and handed it to Clay. "Along with a few articles of clothing, these are Catalina's belongings."

Clay opened it, revealing a couple of letters, a prayer book, a pearl necklace, a black onyx ring and a photograph. He stared at the contents for the longest time, then pulled out the photograph and handed it to Dani.

She immediately recognized Clay and the airplane they'd traveled on. The young man, she suspected, was his son, Trevor.

"Those items now belong to the child," the priest said.

Clay cleared his throat, but didn't speak. He didn't have to. Grief and remorse stretched across his face, and Dani's heart went out to him.

At the sound of footsteps, Dani glanced to the doorway that led to the hall and watched the nun carry in an infant wrapped in a nondescript, white flannel blanket.

"As you can see," the padre said, nodding toward the sleeping baby, "she isn't much bigger than a newborn, but from what her mother inscribed in the prayer book, she was born more than three months ago."

The nun tried to hand the baby to Clay, but he shook his head and took a step back.

Dani reached for the child, drawing her close and holding her gently. Then she carefully pulled back the flannel blanket to reveal the little face.

She could feel Clay's gaze and the intensity of his interest. He might not be comfortable holding an infant but he was studying her even more closely than Dani was.

The baby had pretty features, with a head of black hair, a perfect little nose and lips. But she peered at Dani with lifeless eyes. No spark of interest, no connection.

"I'm not sure what's wrong," the padre said. "She doesn't respond to anyone."

"Is she deaf or blind?" Clay asked, apparently picking up the same something-isn't-right vibe that Dani had sensed.

"I don't think so," the priest said. "If you clap your hands loud, she'll turn to the noise. But I've read about cases like this, where a child is raised without love or compassion. Some children can die from lack of human contact."

Would she ever recover? Dani was afraid to ask, afraid to consider the possibility. She glanced at Clay, saw the same concern, the same questions rising in his eyes.

"What's her name?" Clay asked.

"I don't believe Catalina gave her one. And Manuela only referred to her as...well, she didn't call her by name."

Dani hoped Clay came up with something fitting—and soon. The poor baby had been neglected too long already.

"I'll call her Angela," he said, his deep voice almost a whisper.

Dani ran her finger along the child's cheek. "It's a beautiful name, and fitting for a precious little angel who has been ignored for way too long."

"Angela was also my mother's name," Clay added, his eyes focused on the baby.

"By the way," the priest said. "She hasn't been

christened. I'd be happy to do that for you, if you would like me to."

Dani looked at Clay, wondering how he'd answer. After all, she had no idea if he was a religious man.

"Yes, we'll do that before we leave." Then he nodded toward the front door. "Can you and I take a little walk, Padre? I'd like to talk to you about something. In private."

Dani wasn't sure what he planned to discuss with the priest, and although curious, she let them go. All that seemed to matter to her right now was the child and getting her to a doctor as soon as possible.

As Clay walked the grounds of the small church with the priest, his boots crunched along the graveled path. "I want you to know how much I appreciate you stepping in and taking the baby from that woman. Just from what you've shared I'd side with those calling her a witch."

Padre Luis nodded. "I must admit that I was worried when I learned the baby had been left in Manuela's care. But I am also a man who believes in miracles. I hoped that having a little one in the house would soften her heart, but that didn't happen. Believe me, *señor.* The moment I sensed the baby was in danger, I convinced Manuela to give her to the church."

Clay wished the padre had figured it out sooner, but there wasn't anything he could do about that now. "I want to take the baby with me today. I'd like to have her examined by a doctor in Texas as soon as possible."

"You don't question the fact that she is your flesh and blood?" the priest asked.

"Most men would, I suppose." Clay would have a DNA test run when he got home. But for now he had all the proof he needed. The ring in Catalina's box had belonged to Trevor. Clay had given it to him as a graduation gift. And the photograph had been taken the day Clay had purchased the King Air.

Trevor had been excited when Clay traded in the old Cessna for the new plane, and he'd planned to get certified in the King Air, but when word came through that he'd been accepted into the study abroad program, he decided to put it off until he returned from Guadalajara.

Clay hadn't been keen on the boy leaving. He'd never felt comfortable in Mexico himself; although Trevor spoke Spanish fluently and wasn't the kind of kid to get into trouble.

Trevor had looked forward to the trip and the year he would be away. Once he was settled, he called home periodically with updates about the university, his studies and the charm of the city and the people he'd met, especially a young woman he'd started dating.

During a couple of those calls, Trevor had asked Clay to fly to Guadalajara and visit, but…

Clay chuffed. But he'd never gotten around to it.

"I don't suppose you'll have any trouble getting the baby out of Mexico," the padre said. "But taking her into the United States may be difficult."

Clay knew that. "Do you have a birth certificate for her? Something that proves she's Trevor's daughter?"

The priest shook his head. "The baby was born at Manuela's house, and she never filed the necessary papers. But having her christened here at the church will give you some documents to prove her birth."

"That woman ought to be locked up," Clay said, unwilling to let it drop. "How could someone neglect a baby like that?"

"There are some in town who would agree with you," the priest said. "But speaking of the baby, I have another idea. Why don't I write a letter for you to take to the American Consulate? I can declare the child was given up to the church for adoption."

"Will that help?"

The old man smiled. "In itself? Perhaps not." He pointed a crooked finger toward the clouds and beyond. "But I have a little—what do you Americans call it?—a little pull?"

Clay had a feeling they were going to need all the *pull* they could get—heavenly or otherwise.

His only other option was to send Roger and Dani home on a commercial flight. No need for either of them to risk getting into trouble with the authorities. Then he could fly his plane home, taking the baby with him. He'd just claim the child was his.

Hell, as far as he was concerned, the baby *was* his. And she, Angela, was going to wither up and die if he didn't get her home and under the care of a doctor. Each time he looked into her empty eyes it tore an aching hole in his chest.

Clay reached into his pocket and withdrew his wallet, where he kept a personal check. "Do you have a pen, Padre?"

"Yes, I do." The priest patted himself, then pulled one out of a pocket in his black jacket. "Here you go."

Clay stopped near a picnic table, then scratched out a check in appreciation. "Thank you for looking after the baby for me."

The priest looked at the check, squinted, then glanced up at Clay. "This is a lot of money, *señor.*"

"Thanks for rescuing my…baby."

"Well," the priest said, folding the check and placing it in his pocket, "why don't we go back and have your daughter christened?"

"Whatever you say, Padre."

They stopped at the house long enough to round up Dani and the baby, then headed back to the small church, where Angela Catalina Callaghan was welcomed into God's family. Clay wasn't big on religion, but he had a feeling he'd disappointed the

Old Boy upstairs on many occasions. This time he'd decided to do things right.

Angela seemed oblivious to the whole process, and when it was over, the priest filled out a baptismal record and handed it to Clay. Then he returned to his office to compose the letter.

In the meantime, Dani and Clay took a walk outdoors. She carried the baby, but he continued to steal a peek at the little one, hoping to see a spark of life, a glimmer of hope in her eyes. He wasn't sure what he was looking for, but it clearly wasn't there.

Clay glanced at his watch, eager to get his granddaughter home, where he would do whatever it took, pay whatever it cost, to get her the best American doctors, the best therapists—whatever she needed.

And he wasn't about to waste another minute.

He glanced at the paper the priest had given him, hoping it would be enough to offer the American authorities. It was all in Spanish, but he could decipher most of it.

"Well, I'll be damned," he muttered. Things were looking up, and if his luck held, he'd have the baby back in Houston tonight. He shot a glance at Dani. "As soon as Padre Luis gives us that letter, we're getting out of here. We need to get back to the hotel."

"Why's that? There are a lot of things to do yet, and we need to speak to someone at the consulate."

"I plan to be home before dark."

"You can't leave that soon," Dani told him.

"Yes I can. I'm getting that baby out of here, even if I have to put you and Roger on a commercial flight and fly her home myself."

"You're going to pilot the plane?" she asked.

"I'm certified."

"Just what are you going to tell the authorities in Houston?" she asked.

"That Angela is my daughter. That she and I flew to Guadalajara to visit with family. While in her aunt's care, she became sick, and I'm taking her home."

"You don't have a birth certificate for her," Dani reminded him.

He pulled out the baptismal certificate listing him as the child's father. Her eyes widened. "You asked a priest to lie on your behalf?"

"No. He just made a mistake, and I didn't correct him. Besides, financially speaking, I'm raising this child. And I'll be the one answering to 'Daddy.' As soon as I get home, I'll make things legal."

She slapped her hands on her hips. "I can't believe this is happening. You intend to whisk her back to Texas without going through the proper channels?"

"I intend to get her to a doctor in the States."

"Well, if you're so smart and have this all figured out, why the hell did you drag an attorney down here?"

"I needed an interpreter," he fired back. "And someone to get my ass out of jail if anyone tried to stop me from taking my kid home."

"Oh, for goodness sake. You're talking about having your plane confiscated, a ten-thousand-dollar fine and jail time." Dani placed her fingers against her temples and kneaded the budding headache Clay Callaghan had sprung upon her. The hardheaded man was going to drive her batty.

She took a deep breath, then puffed it out. "Slow down, Clay. I understand why we need to get her home. And quickly. But let me make a few calls. I'll claim a medical emergency and extenuating circumstances. Maybe I can expedite the process."

He studied her for a moment, eyes drilling into her.

"You'd better work some kind of miracle," Clay said. "Because this baby is going home within the next twelve hours…one way or another."

After the new bottles they'd brought from Houston had been washed and boiled, Dani changed the baby's diapers, then dressed her in one of the pink sleepers they'd purchased at Spend-Mart. Unfortunately, since Dani hadn't known the baby's age or size, little Angela swam in the outfit.

Next she opened the can of formula and prepared a bottle. She suspected Angela was hungry, because she fussed and squirmed.

When Delia, Dani's younger sister, had been a

baby, she'd screamed her head off whenever she was hungry, wet or bothered by something. But perhaps that was because her cries were always answered, her needs always met.

As Dani sat on the sofa at the priest's house, she wrapped the blanket around Angela, swaddling her and holding her close. Then she again offered the baby the bottle.

Angela finally took the nipple, sucking down the formula, and Dani brushed a finger across her little cheek. "That a girl. We've got more where this came from. And we'll have you filled out and healthy before you know it."

At the sound of footsteps, she looked up and spotted Clay. His eyes locked on hers, and the intensity of his gaze was hard to ignore. In the silence a hundred thoughts tumbled between them, one of which was the difference of opinion they had when it came to getting the baby out of Mexico legally. Yet they also had a common goal. A concern for Angela.

"What do you think?" he asked. "Has she been abused as well as neglected?"

"I didn't see any bruises or marks on her when I changed her," Dani said. "I have the feeling that, for the most part, she was left to cry until it didn't seem necessary to bother."

"I'd like to throttle that woman," he said.

"Me, too," Dani admitted. "But that wouldn't do us any good. And it would most likely land you in jail."

"I'm glad Martin sent you with me," he said, his voice softening and causing something warm to build and topple inside her. "Your experience with kids has come in handy."

She stiffened. Did he know about…?

"Don't worry, Dani. I'm not going to mention anything to Martin about that."

A memory surfaced, and the words they'd shared after the sobering, blood-stirring kiss came to mind.

Martin will—

It was no big deal, Dani. It'll be our secret. No one will ever find out.

Clay raked a hand through his hair, as if his thoughts had drifted in the same direction.

The scent of his musky cologne, the slick velvety softness of his mouth, the way his hands stroked the curve of her back, the slope of her derriere. The hardness of his arousal when he had pulled her hips against him.

He cleared his throat. "I'm going to tell the driver we'll be leaving shortly."

She nodded, then watched him go. As the door shut behind him, the nun, Maria Teresa, entered the room.

"How's the baby doing?" she asked in Spanish.

"She's eating very well," Dani answered, also in Spanish. She glanced down at Angela and saw that the bottle was nearly empty. "You'll never be hungry again, little one."

For a moment Angela looked at her. *Really looked.* Then the emptiness in her eyes returned. But there had been a connection, slight as it was, a spark of some kind. Dani would swear to it.

"Ay, Dios mio," the nun whispered.

"Did you see it, too?" Dani asked in her native tongue.

Maria Teresa nodded. "I have been praying that God would provide a mother for her."

Surely the nun didn't think that Dani and Clay were a couple. Or that Dani was the nanny who would be mothering this child. Not that Dani didn't like children. They were fine in small doses. But at the ripe old age of twenty-five, she was all mothered out. Besides, she and God had made a pact. Once Delia was eighteen and had gone on to college, Dani would be free. Clay had yet to hire someone to look after the baby, but Dani would suggest he find a loving, competent, maternal woman who enjoyed kids.

"Es un milagro," the nun said, proclaiming a miracle. Then she turned and left the house.

Dani suspected she'd gone to tell the padre what they both may or may not have witnessed. But the well-intentioned woman had jumped the gun and come to the wrong conclusion. The baby's brief response had merely been a sign of hope raising the possibility that Angela *might* get better, that she *might* begin to connect and respond to the person holding her.

And that person should be Clay.

He obviously wasn't comfortable with infants; after all, he'd claimed not to have held his son until the boy was two. But Clay would have to get over that. And quickly.

Dani was a career woman with a job to do. Once she managed to get this child out of Mexico—legally—she would find a way to force Clay to take an active role in Angela's daily care. In the meantime Dani was merely a temporary babysitter who already had three too many kids to look after. And for the next twelve years.

It wasn't so long, she supposed, but it seemed like forever right now. Still, one day she'd be free to live a life of her own.

Once upon a time, romantic, family-oriented dreams had simmered deep in her heart, but as her responsibilities for and her obligations to her siblings steadily grew, so did a determination to create her own happily-ever-after.

She'd be pushing forty then, and too tired of kids to consider a family of her own. Not that she had any regrets about that.

Why should she?

Her thoughts drifted back to her own brood, the kids she'd left in Houston. She'd managed to appease the younger two, but they weren't the ones she was worried about. Sara, the oldest, was going through a rebellious stage and could revolt at any moment.

For that reason, Dani whispered a prayer.

Hopefully, the headstrong teen wasn't giving Mrs. Fuentes any trouble.

Chapter Five

Deep in the heart of Houston, Sara de la Cruz sat on her twin bed in the small, cramped bedroom she shared with her younger sister and stared out the window at the world she'd been denied.

The door to her room was closed, with the dresser shoved in place to keep everyone out, yet that didn't seem to stop Marcos, who continued to knock loudly.

"Mrs. Fuentes said you've been in there long enough, Sara, and it's time to come out. Besides, breakfast is ready."

In response, Sara turned up the volume of the radio. She was so angry she could scream. First of all, her whole summer was ruined because Dani had made her stay home and look after Marcos and Delia. But then, when Dani had to fly to Mexico on business, she'd hired a babysitter—which, by the way, she could never afford before.

So where had all the money come from?

Did Dani think Sara was stupid? Attorneys made tons of money. Everyone knew that. So there was only one reason Dani would insist Sara stay home and help out with the kids. She was mean. She didn't want Sara to have a life or get a summer vacation.

But even if that wasn't the case—how come she had to hire Mrs. Fuentes to come over and babysit? Didn't she trust Sara to stay alone at night? Or did she think Sara wasn't responsible enough to feed the kids dinner, make them take a bath and put them to bed?

Sara gave a frustrated sigh, then bent forward to pluck at a loose green thread on the worn Barbie bedspread that was *so* not cool.

"We'll redo your bedroom next month," Dani had said.

Yeah, yeah, yeah.

A strand of Sara's long, black hair slid forward and brushed against her cheek. She flicked it back over her shoulder and swore under her breath. It was *so* not fair.

She hated being treated like a little kid. She was fourteen years old, a teenager and practically an adult.

It sucked having a sitter.

Sheesh.

"Come on, you guys," Dani had said yesterday when she dropped the bomb on them. "I don't want to go, but I have to. My boss needs me in Mexico on business."

Yeah, right.

She was probably off on some vacation, having fun and getting a break from the kids, while Sara was locked up in this house. Well, Sara was through being a doormat, through being stuck at home during the day, then treated like a baby at night.

She climbed off the bed, then dug through the closet until she found the canvas tote bag she used on those rare occasions when she was allowed to sleep over at a friend's house. After pulling it out and dumping the leftover crumbs of a granola bar onto the floor, she packed it with a couple of outfits Dani didn't approve of: the jeans with the frayed hems and the T-shirt that had fit kind of loose last year, but was smaller now and made the guys all stare and grin at her.

Marcos banged on the door again. "Don't be a stubborn brat, Sara. You're going to starve to death, and see if I care."

For a moment she paused, catching the aroma of bacon and a faint whiff of hotcakes and maple syrup. A pang of hunger made her momentarily reconsider. But instead she reached for the top shelf in the closet, where she'd hidden a half-eaten bag of barbecue potato chips from Marcos so he couldn't wolf 'em all down.

She wouldn't starve to death. She had friends who appreciated her, friends who weren't allowed at the house while she babysat her brother and sister, which was every dang day.

But those days were over.

She'd show Dani that she couldn't be bossed around anymore.

As soon as Dani had fed the baby, she called Ray Martinez, a former classmate from law school and a topnotch attorney who'd gotten a great position with the State Department.

Clay seemed to appreciate her efforts, but he hadn't sat idly by and waited to see what she might accomplish. Instead he got busy himself. The first thing he'd done was purchase two first-class tickets on a commercial flight from Guadalajara to Houston for Dani and Roger.

She was on hold, but when she realized what he was doing, she covered the mouthpiece and whispered, "You're not flying back alone."

"You're right. I'll have the baby with me."

She knew what he was thinking. If there were any problems in Houston, he'd be the only one in the hot seat. "Trust me on this, will you, Clay?"

"I'm not big on trusting someone else to solve my problems for me."

She wanted to clobber him. Never had she snapped at a client. Never had she allowed a man to rile her so. But Clay Callaghan would try the patience of a saint. "Damn it, Clay. I'm trying to solve *potential* problems."

"You just swore in a priest's house. Isn't that a mortal sin or something?" He tossed her a grin much like Marcos did when he was being mischievous, the exasperating kind that made a woman laugh when it would feel so much better to be spitting mad.

She'd never met a client who could cause her to lose her balance, as this one had.

Last night he'd kissed her senseless. And today he was making her crazy.

"I won't let you take that risk," she said, realizing there wasn't much she could do about it, other than stomp, scream and curse. And, yes, doing something like that in a priest's house seemed unforgivable.

"Dani?" Ray asked, coming back on the line. "I'll call you back."

"All right." She ended the call.

When Clay called the hotel to speak to Roger, telling him about the change in plans, Dani's patience was wearing thin. "Would you just let me have the time to do the job you hired me to do?"

"This is only a backup plan. I always have one."

She suspected he did, but there were holes in his secondary strategy.

When Ray's call came in, she grabbed it on the first ring. "Yes?"

"You owe me," Ray said. "And I *don't* mean dinner."

"Thank God." She glanced at Clay, then made a circle with her index finger and thumb. "Right now I'd almost agree to anything, Ray."

A couple of years ago, she and Ray Martinez had tiptoed around a relationship, but the timing had never been right.

She supposed Ray was still interested, but she had way too many responsibilities at home to even consider going out to dinner with anyone, let alone striking up a romance. How could she expect a man to want to take on three kids?

When she disconnected the line, she tossed a smug smile at her exasperating client—a stubborn rancher who stirred her senses in one passionate response or another. "We've got a temporary visa. All we need to do is pick it up at the American Consulate."

A slow grin tugged at Clay's mouth, and his eyes glimmered with...what? Admiration? Respect? Something else?

"You owe me," she said.

And I don't mean dinner, came to mind. But she clamped her mouth shut.

In less than two hours' time, the paperwork had been walked through the proper channels, and Clay had been granted permission to bring Angela back to Houston—legally. The entire adoption process could take a year or more, but for now they were on track and scheduled to leave Mexico with the approval of both countries.

If God had granted a miracle today, that was it.

Dani didn't care what the nun had said. Any connection Dani may have made with the baby would end as soon as she got back to the States. Clay was the one who would need to bond with the poor little orphan…and quickly.

When it came time to leave Guadalajara, Clay offered Dani the commercial ticket. She'd been tempted to take it, but her reputation was at stake. After whatever had—or hadn't—happened yesterday, she needed to prove herself. And the only way to do that was to return home on the same little plane she'd arrived in—without panicking or having a single drop of alcohol. Then maybe she'd leave Clay with a better impression of her.

So she boarded the King Air with all the courage she could muster, reminding herself that Roger had seemed to be a competent pilot.

Once she'd taken a seat, Clay asked, "Can I get you a drink?"

"No, thank you. I'll ride this one out." She wasn't about to put herself at a disadvantage. Besides, holding the baby had a calming effect on her, giving her something to think about, someone else to focus on.

About fifteen minutes into the flight, she asked Clay if he'd like to hold Angela.

"No. I'll wait until she's bigger. And healthier."

"She scares you," Dani said, watching the tough-as-cowhide Texas cattleman stiffen and tense in his seat.

"I'm not afraid of anything. I'm just not comfortable with babies."

He'd made that clear yesterday. "You said that you weren't around Trevor when he was young."

"I wasn't."

"Did you divorce his mother when he was a baby?"

"I never married her."

"Why not?" The moment the question slid out, she wished she could reel it back in. That was none of her business—no matter how curious she might be.

His gaze met hers, and she watched a struggle unfold in his expression. She had a feeling he wasn't the kind to open up and share personal thoughts. And right about the time she was going to apologize for prying, he shrugged and relaxed in his seat.

"Sally was a city girl and the niece of another rancher in town. She was spending the summer in Texas. She was bored, and I helped fill her days."

"It was just a fling," Dani said, making the assumption.

"Yeah, I suppose. Things started out hot and wild for a while, but by the end of the summer they'd pretty much fizzled out. Unfortunately she ended up getting pregnant."

"Did she want to get married?"

"She'd already gotten involved with someone else." Clay's gaze zeroed in on her. "Like I said, it was just one of those things."

Hot and brief.

She thought of the kiss she and Clay had shared, the heat that had threatened to consume them—if she had let it. Of course, it was all over and done with now.

So why did the kiss continue to dog her when other memories of yesterday didn't?

"Sally ended up marrying a guy from her hometown," Clay said, "and I was okay with that. We settled on a fair amount of child support, and I sent a check monthly."

"Did you get to see Trevor at all?"

"She came out to visit her uncle when Trevor was two. And after that, once he got in school, he came to stay with me a couple of weeks in the summer. But one day, when he was about fourteen, Sally called me and asked if I'd take him. She'd gotten divorced and had hooked up with some new guy who didn't like having a kid around, even one who was half-grown."

"Did you take him?"

"Hell, yes." Clay appeared to be offended, as though she'd challenged some ethical code he ascribed to.

She tried to get a handle on the type of man Clay

Callaghan was. Duty-bound, she supposed. But not at all in touch with his emotions.

She glanced at Angela. Having a baby around would certainly change things for him.

Hopefully.

Maybe she ought to help things along.

While Angela slept, Dani unhooked her seat belt, then stood.

"What are you doing?" Clay asked.

"Here." She placed the baby in his lap, then plopped back in her seat.

"What the hell did you do that for?"

"Because you'd better get used to holding her."

"I'll *never* get used to it."

"That's what I thought about flying. And look at me now. I'm becoming an old hand at this." She held out her fingers, showed him how they trembled only a little. "So the sooner you start holding her, the better. You're going to be her father."

"Maybe, but I'm a lousy dad. If Trevor was still here, he'd tell you."

"What would he say?" she asked, trying to draw him out. Not that she wanted to hear of his failures. She knew exactly how he felt, since she and Sara had started butting heads. She also knew that he needed the confidence to try again.

Clay shrugged, his eyes traveling to the sleeping baby in his arms.

"Do you have any family nearby?" Dani asked.

"Maybe a mother or sister who can step in and help you with her?"

"I was an only child, and my mom died when I was ten."

"I'm sorry."

"Yeah. It was tough. She was pretty sick the last few months."

"What about your dad?"

"He took off long before that."

"Who raised you?"

"Rex Billings, the man who used to own my ranch. He was close to seventy when I first met him. He was also a hard-ass cowboy who taught me to be tough and to be a man. And as far as I'm concerned, he was my dad."

Dani suspected the old cowboy had done too good of a job teaching Clay to be tough. "So did he help you with Trevor?"

"No, he was gone by the time Trevor started coming to visit."

"Gone?" she asked.

"Rex used to hang out at the café where my mom used to work. When her cancer progressed to the point she couldn't work anymore, we got evicted, and so Rex took us in. When I was twenty-two, he had a heart attack in his sleep. Even though it came as a surprise, he couldn't have asked for a better way to go.

"How about you?" he asked. "Was your old man good to you?"

"He was the best," she said, her voice getting a bit wobbly, like it did each time she talked about her father.

They sat in silence for a while, and she suspected Clay would have been content with that. But the conversation would help her to keep her mind off the flight and off the clock.

"How did Trevor end up in Mexico?" she asked.

"He was attending the university there as part of an international study program." Clay grew still. Quiet. Introspective.

Martin had said Clay's son had died in an automobile accident, although Dani didn't know the details and was reluctant to ask.

"I know you're not comfortable with small babies," she said. "But that's the hand you've been dealt. I admire you for taking on the responsibility, but you're going to have to put that child's emotional needs ahead of your own."

"I don't have emotional needs."

"Yes you do. Everyone does."

He scoffed. "I have feelings, if that's what you mean."

"I'm sure you do. But that baby needs someone to connect with, so keeping your distance will do more harm than good."

"I thought you were an attorney, but you sound like a shrink."

"I like to think of it as having common sense."

As Angela began to wake, Clay tensed. "Here, you'd better take her."

"Hang on. Let me fix a bottle."

Clay scrunched his face, but held the baby, trying to shush her.

Purposely Dani took her time, hoping he'd look into Angela's eyes and see the same spark she'd seen. Hoping Angela would recognize the man who would be her daddy, who'd make sure all her needs were met.

"I know that I got angry when you were dead-set on bringing her home any way you could," she said, "but I want you to know that I admire you for it, too."

"It's the least I can do for her father. I let Trevor down as a kid. And when he died, it tore a big hole in my life."

She suspected it had broken Clay's heart, too, even if he didn't mention it.

"This is going to be tough on me," he told her. "I've always been a loner."

"Having kids around does complicate things," she said, drawing on her own experience. "But it can be rewarding, too."

He shot her a skeptical look. When she'd filled the bottle with formula and screwed on the nipple, he handed her the baby.

Dani's heart went out to the Marlboro Man, and she realized they had something in common. On the outside they had the world at their feet. But on the inside he wasn't any more prepared to raise this baby than she was to raise the brood she'd inherited.

In just a little over three hours, the King Air landed in Houston—safe and sound. And thanks to Dani's efforts to secure the proper paperwork, they strolled through customs without a hitch.

After leaving Roger at the airport and adjusting the car seat in the back seat of Clay's dual-wheeled pickup, they headed to town.

Dani was eager to get to the office, where she'd left her car, then go home. Since the trip had taken less time than she'd expected, the kids were going to be surprised to see her.

"Do you mind going with me to the pediatrician's office?" Clay asked.

Yes and no. In part, she wanted to hear a doctor's prognosis for the baby. But she was also pressed to get home, see about the kids and pay Mrs. Fuentes so she could be on her way.

"What time is the appointment?" she asked.

"What appointment? Do I need one?"

Was he serious? "Of course you need one. You can't just show up at a doctor's office without calling first."

"Well, hell," he said. "I didn't know that. The last time I saw a doctor was when I fell off a horse and broke my arm in two places."

"How old were you?"

"Eleven or twelve."

"And Rex didn't call first?"

"Nope. Took me right in and told someone to set it."

Was there anything Clay thought a demanding personality couldn't achieve or money couldn't buy? Before she lost her head and snapped back at one of the firm's top clients, she caught herself. How could this man do that to her? Get her all riled up in a heartbeat?

"Can you recommend a pediatrician?" he asked.

All right. So it was growing more apparent that she'd mentioned the kids to him when she'd been tipsy. She hoped his no-tell philosophy in regard to Martin also included the fact that she wasn't as career focused as she'd like to be.

"Dr. Baker has a great reputation," she said. "And he stays late on Wednesdays to offer an alternative to working parents. But just in case he's too busy to fit us in, we can take her to the emergency room at the hospital. Someone will be able to see us there." Dani reached into her purse and pulled out her cell. She dialed the number she'd come to know as well as her own.

Within minutes they had an appointment to see the pediatrician at six forty-five.

"They'll squeeze us in," she said.

"Good."

While she had her phone out, she dialed home, and Mrs. Fuentes answered on the second ring.

"Hello?"

"Hi, Sofia. It's me. How is everything going?"

"Not so good. Sara's been gone since early this morning. For a while I thought she ran away. But Marcos followed her and found her at a friend's house. Someone named Jessica, I think. And she's still there."

Oh, God. What next?

"I'll be home in twenty minutes," she told the sitter. Then she turned to Clay. "I'm sorry. I can't go with you. I've got problems at home."

"What's wrong?"

Dani's first inclination had been to shrug off his question. She'd never shared her fears or insecurities with anyone before, but for some reason Clay's concern touched her, and she wondered just what she'd told him last night in Guadalajara.

Too much already, she suspected. But the fact that he'd confided how he felt, that he believed he'd failed with his son made it easier to share.

"I'd asked Sara to stick around the house until I got home. But apparently, she took off."

"Which one is Sara?" he asked.

"The teenager. She's been complaining about not having enough freedom." Dani let out a soft sigh. "I'm sure you know how adolescents are. I swear, girls have to be the worst at that age."

"Actually," Clay admitted, "I don't know squat about kids—especially adolescent girls. And I damn sure don't have any advice. If I'd gone against one of Rex's orders, he'd have come unglued and cussed a blue streak."

"Yeah, well Sara can really push my buttons. A couple of times I've come close to losing control of my tongue."

"Maybe she needs a trip to the woodshed," Clay said.

"I can't spank her. She's too big for that."

"Hell, it was just a joke. Rex never laid a hand on me. But then, I always appreciated what he was trying to do."

"I was a good kid, too," Dani told him. "I tried to do whatever I could to make things easier on my parents."

A light at the intersection turned red, and when Clay braked to a stop, he glanced across the seat, his gaze snagging hers and offering the first bit of compassion she'd received in what seemed like forever. "But Sara's not like you."

"That's for sure. I'm at my wit's end." Dani sighed again. "If my dad were still alive, this wouldn't have happened. He always knew what to say to her, and I only seem to set her off."

"Maybe it's because you're too close in age."

"You might be right. The sad thing is that we used to be so close. Now all we do is fight."

A tear slipped down Dani's face, and she swiped it away, cursing her weakness under her breath. "I'm sorry. This is so hard. And I'm pedaling as fast as I can."

Clay reached across the seat and cupped her jaw, his callused thumb brushing at the moisture on her cheek. "You're doing a hell of a job trying to keep your family together. Don't let a snot-nosed kid who's just ten years out of a diaper tell you otherwise."

She grinned. "Thanks, Clay."

They stayed like that, connected by something intangible. Attraction, arousal.

That hot, tantalizing kiss they'd shared came to mind.

The memory simmered between them until some idiot behind them honked his horn, letting them know the light had turned green.

"Where does this Jessica live?" Clay asked, as he continued down the highway.

"Why do you ask?"

"I'm going with you."

She ought to have been embarrassed dragging him into her family situation. She should tell him to forget it and demand he return her to the office so she could get her car and handle things on her own.

But it had seemed like forever since she'd had anyone in her corner. And right now the rugged rancher, who, by his own admission, had been a lousy parent, was all she had.

Chapter Six

Clay maneuvered his truck down the quiet street where Sara's friend lived, hoping he hadn't bitten off more than he could chew.

He didn't get involved in other people's business. Never had. Never meant to this time.

"You didn't have to come along," Dani said.

He knew that. "Let's just say I owe you one."

"That's okay. I was only doing my job."

He glanced across the seat at his traveling companion, who was dressed casually yet professionally, in a pair of black slacks and a jacket. A cream-colored knit top and a single pearl on a silver necklace completed the ensemble. She'd been wearing it all day, and it still looked nice. Or rather, she still looked nice.

"This is above and beyond the call of duty," she added.

The last thing in the world he wanted to do was to get involved in Dani's personal problems, but he wasn't up for a visit to the pediatrician, either. At least, not by himself. So he'd do whatever it took to make sure Dani was free to accompany him.

Okay. So his motives were selfish. And even though he hadn't offered to do anything other than drive her there, he wanted to see the wild child back on track so Dani could focus on Angela.

There wasn't much he could do personally, though. Other than offer the kid—Sara—a couple of hundred dollars to straighten up and behave herself. When all else failed, money seemed to be a powerful motivator for some folks. In fact, maybe he ought to cut to the chase and just offer the cash right off the bat.

He patted the pocket of his blue-plaid shirt and felt the folded hundred dollar bills he'd stuck there to use as bribes in Mexico, if he'd needed them. After making sure they were still there, he glanced at his wristwatch—5:46. There was still time before their appointment, but Clay figured they would be in and out of the doctor's office quicker if they arrived early. Of course, they couldn't do anything until Sara was back home and compliant.

Ten minutes later Dani instructed him to park in front of a pale-yellow house on a quiet street.

"Wait here. I'll be right back." She climbed from the truck and headed for the front door.

He watched as she stood on the porch and knocked.

Before long, a teenage girl with shoulder-length blond hair answered the door. She nodded, then looked over her shoulder and called someone. As the blonde stepped back into the house, a sullen-faced young lady with long, black hair came outside. He spotted a family resemblance and assumed she was Dani's sister.

Every once in a while the girl glanced at Clay, at his pickup. Each time she did, he smiled. But patience wasn't one of his strong points, and he forced himself to sit back and wait for Dani to convince her sister to get in the truck.

As Dani stepped away from the house, Sara closed the door and joined her on the lawn.

Clay didn't mean to eavesdrop, but the window was down on the truck, and now that they'd stepped away from the house, he overheard their conversation.

"I came to pick you up," Dani said.

"Well, I'm not ready to go yet."

"I'm not sure what you're trying to do here, Sara. But it's not fair."

"What do you know about being fair?" Sara

snapped. "You're able to leave the house whenever *you* want. But I'm stuck babysitting. And then, when I would have been happy to help you out, you hire a sitter for *me*. *Me*. And I'm almost an adult."

"Sara," Dani said, keeping her cool. "Let's talk about this at home."

The surly teen crossed her arms. "I'm sick and tired of staying at home. I want a life, just like all my friends have. Darn it, Dani, summer is practically over."

"I'm sorry that you've had to take on additional responsibility," Dani said. "But I need you to cooperate a little while longer."

Until she was eighteen, Clay thought.

"You know what really hurts?" Sara asked. "You can't afford to hire someone to watch over the kids when I want to go someplace, but you can find the money when you want to go to Mexico." The teen's gaze drifted to the truck again and to Clay, then she slapped her hands on her hips. "And you *said* you were working…"

"I *was* working, little girl."

"Oh, yeah?" the teen asked, nodding her head toward Clay. "Well, he's not dressed in a suit like those other guys at the office. If you ask me, he looks like a date."

A grin tugged at Clay's lips. He did, huh? He wondered what Sara would say if she knew about the blood-rushing, conscience-battering kiss he and her big sister had shared last night.

"I'm not dating Mr. Callaghan," Dani said, her own hands plopping onto her hips and entering a face-off she'd have to fight to win.

"Well maybe you *should*," her sister said. "Maybe you'd be nicer and not so bossy."

"Oh, for Pete's sake," Dani said. "Believe it or not, that man waiting patiently for us in his truck is my client. We were coming home from the airport when I got word that you jumped ship."

Sara studied Clay as though she was still stuck on the dating stuff, then crossed her arms and shifted her weight to one foot. "Whatever. You don't understand how hard it is for me at home. Marcos does everything he can to annoy me. And Delia follows me around everywhere I go, even to the bathroom. They're making my life miserable, and you don't even care."

"I do care," Dani said. "It's difficult for me, too. But right now, we all have to do our part."

"That's easy for you to say," the teenager complained. "You're never home."

Dani's lips tightened and her right eye twitched. He sensed her frustration and anger, and not just because he was siding with an adult over a mouthy teenager who probably could benefit from a spanking, whether she was too old or not.

Yesterday, while Dani had been jabbering on the plane, she'd mentioned the medical bills, the mortgage and the student loans she was trying to repay. He suspected the financial stress would start lifting soon, now that she had a position with Phillips, Crowley and Norman. But if her problems at home began to affect her work, she could lose her job. Then where would she be?

The baby started to whimper, and Clay suspected she was wet or hungry or something. And he didn't know what to do about it.

So in spite of a reluctance to get involved, he opened the door and stepped out of the truck. At his approach, the teen grew silent.

"Sara?" he asked.

She nodded, eyes wide and lips parted.

He reached out a hand. "I'm Clay Callaghan. I own a ranch about thirty miles from here. Somehow I feel as though I owe you an apology."

The stunned teen placed a hand on her chest. "Me?"

Good. He'd caught her off guard. He nodded toward the pickup. "There's a baby in there, and we're on the way to see a doctor to have her checked out. She was stuck in Mexico for three months, and your sister, who is my attorney, helped me cut through the legal crap and bring her home."

She glanced at the dual-wheeled black truck, then at Clay, her eyes traveling from his boots to his hat. She wasn't very tall, so she had to lean back to look him in the eye.

Dani had said she was too big to spank, and he

had to agree. But he'd be damned if he knew how to deal with teenage girls, especially when they were being selfish and emotional. Still, he'd felt compelled to jump right into the midst of a private family crisis. And now that he had, he had to think fast.

"Do you mind if I talk to you?" he asked the girl. "Alone?"

The question hung in the air, as both young women gawked at him.

Okay, they were a bit dumbfounded by his comment.

So was he.

But the ploy, as much hot wind as it held, seemed to be working because Sara glanced at her sister for some kind of validation, yet all Dani had been able to do was gape at him.

"The baby's hungry," Clay told her, giving her an out. "And I'm not sure what to do with her, remember?"

A yes seemed to squeak out of her parted lips. Flustered yet kissable lips. Then he turned to her sister.

"Come on. Let's take a walk." He placed a hand on Sara's shoulder, slowly guiding her toward the street.

Taking a ride, a drive or a walk had been one of Rex's old ploys. A parental technique that put a spin on a visit to the woodshed, although the old man had never laid a hand on Clay—either in anger or affection.

When Clay glanced over his shoulder at Dani, she appeared to be mesmerized by his actions. Of course, she couldn't be any more stunned than he was, but there was no need to let her know that. So he winked as he strode off with her younger sister, suggesting he had everything under control, when that couldn't have been any further from the truth.

Dani stood in awe as she watched Clay escort Sara down the street. She had no idea what he was going to tell her, but right now she was thrilled to have reinforcements—even one who, when it came to parenting, was probably questionable at best.

Feeling helpless and at a loss, Dani prepared another bottle, then removed Angela from the car seat.

"She was so sweet as a little girl," Dani whispered to the baby, while offering her the formula.

As usual, the baby seemed to ignore her. Yet that didn't keep Dani from voicing her frustration or her concerns. Somehow, talking out loud seemed to help.

"I try to be patient and tell myself that she's still grieving for our father, not to mention her mom, and that there's no one to lash out at other than me. Believe me, it's tough to lose a parent and to grow up without a mother—*I* know." The truth, and who she'd been speaking to, washed over her. She brushed a kiss across Angela's brow. "You know, too, don't you, sweetheart."

The poor baby had lost both of her parents before getting a chance to know them. To make matters worse, she'd lived for three whole months with a woman who saw her as a curse rather than a blessing.

Dani studied the little face, looking for that spark of connection she'd seen once or possibly twice. She didn't find it this time. Apparently, Angela didn't care one way or the other about being an orphan. And Dani was so much more competent at the office or arguing a case than dealing with traumatized babies or spoiled teenagers.

Parenthood was for the birds.

A little mockingbird came to mind.

You're a real jabberbox, Dani.

That crazy sense of remorse settled over her again, as she struggled to remember what she'd prattled on about yesterday. She normally kept a lot of things locked up inside, and for good reason.

The kids and her insecurity about filling her father's shoes was one of those things, of course. But she had other thoughts and concerns she'd kept to herself. Like the fact that Brian Westlake, one of her co-workers, had been trying to persuade her to go out with him. And he didn't mean dinner.

She knew it was a bad idea to date anyone even remotely connected to the firm, but it had been so long since she'd felt a man's arms around her that she'd been considering it a lot more than she ought to.

It's not as if she had any deep, dark secrets, but she was a person who valued her privacy and kept thoughts and feelings to herself. As it was, she'd been sorry about her inebriation yesterday, but now she *really* rued the decision to drink those stupid screwdrivers, which had made her run off at the mouth and reveal God only knew what to Clay.

So, what had she told him?

She didn't have a clue.

But there was another question she ought to be considering at this time.

What was Clay talking to Sara about?

When Angela had eaten her fill, Dani changed her diaper. She'd no sooner snapped the last button on the baby's little yellow sleeper than she spotted Clay and Sara returning. No tears. No smiles. No apparent tension.

No clues whatsoever.

She tried to ignore her rising curiosity by securing Angela back in the car seat, assuming Clay would want to leave. It was nearing six, and they had a ten-mile drive to Dr. Baker's office. It wasn't that far away, but they had to take Sara home first, and they might hit traffic.

As Clay strode toward the pickup, Sara returned to the house.

Wait just one minute. What had he done? Given her permission to stay? Well, too bad. That wasn't acceptable.

When Clay opened the driver's door, Dani couldn't keep quiet, nor could she control the sarcastic snap in her tone. "Where, pray tell, is she going?"

"To get her bag and tell her friend goodbye."

Just like that?

Dani was momentarily speechless, and before she could quiz Clay about his conversation with the girl, Sara came outdoors carrying a tote bag and made her way to the truck. Clay stood beside his open door, allowing the teenager to slip into the small back seat, next to where Angela was secured in her car seat.

Apparently, Sara had accepted the handsome rancher's correction much better than she ever had Dani's.

Had she found challenging him to be fruitless?

No one spoke on the short drive to Dani's house. When Clay pulled along the curb, Dani addressed her sister for the first time since she'd climbed into the back seat of the pickup.

"Mr. Callaghan would like me to go to Dr. Baker's office with him."

"Yeah," Sara said, as Clay held the door for her to get out. "I know. He told me."

"Can you tell Marcos and Delia that I'll be home shortly? And that I'll take them to the movies."

"Sure."

No complaints? That was surprising.

"You can go, too," Dani told her. "If you'd like. It's your call."

"I'll think about it."

As Sara strode toward the front door, Dani turned to Clay. "What did you do? Bribe her?"

"That crossed my mind. Believe me, I was sorely tempted at first." He shot her a disarming grin. "After hearing her bitch to you, I was also tempted to rip into her and give her hell."

"But you didn't?" Dani asked, wondering what he might have said or done.

"Heck, no. I don't know squat about kids, especially teenage girls. But I decided to treat her like I would any young lady."

Dani wasn't quite following him.

"I gave her more respect than she deserved. I started by calling her Ms. de la Cruz."

"And it worked?"

"It seemed to." His smile dimpled his cheeks, softening him in an appealing way. "I figured that if I treated her like a lady, she'd behave like one."

Dani sat back in her seat and crossed her arms, relief and admiration flooding her chest. "You're a miracle worker."

"I don't know about that." Clay reached into his jacket pocket and pulled out two crisp one-hundred-dollar bills. "It was just an experiment, a half-assed attempt to gain her respect. But if it hadn't worked, I was ready to fork over the cash."

Dani let loose with a nervous giggle that erupted into a stress-relieving laugh. Clay Callaghan was a real novelty and even less prepared to be a parent than she'd been.

But she had to admit he'd scored with Sara. And it hadn't cost him a thing.

At 7:30 Dani and Clay sat in one of several small exam rooms in Dr. Baker's office.

"He's late," Clay muttered. "Our appointment was at 6:45."

"They squeezed us in," she reminded him. "We're lucky to be seen on such short notice."

He scanned the bunny rabbit wallpaper that decorated the room. "I suppose the cutesy decor makes a kid feel better about getting shots and things, huh?"

"That's the idea."

Next he looked at the door, which had a knob set about a foot higher than was standard. "And I'll bet that's so the little rugrats can't escape."

Dani grinned. "Good guess."

A slight rap sounded at the door, before it slowly swung open. Dr. Baker, a balding and bespectacled pediatrician in his midfifties, entered the room. He greeted Dani first, then introduced himself to Clay.

"My nurse told me Angela was born in Mexico," the doctor said.

"Yeah. We just brought her home this afternoon."

The doctor focused on the infant, talking to her first, then slowly beginning a methodical exam.

"Her mother died when she was just a couple of days old," Clay said. "The woman who was supposed to be taking care of her pretty much neglected her, from what we heard."

Thirty minutes later the initial exam revealed that, besides being underweight and slightly malnourished, Angela appeared to be otherwise healthy.

"We're going to take a blood test before you leave, and I'll call you with the results tomorrow afternoon," the doctor said. "But I'm most concerned about her failure to bond. I want to see her again in a week."

Clay shook the man's hand and thanked him.

"The formula you've started her on is all right for now. After seeing the lab results, I may ask you to change it."

After the doctor left, the physician's assistant took blood. The woman was gentle and kind, but the baby cried. When it was all over and Dani reached for her, Angela seemed to focus on the pretty attorney.

Or was that only wishful thinking?

Dani dressed the baby, then picked her up, whispering soothing words. It was at that point Clay began to have second thoughts about taking the kid home alone. Second thoughts? Hell, a sense of panic was setting in. What if something went wrong? What if she cried in the middle of the night?

They left the exam room and stopped by the appointment desk to pay the bill and set up a time for the next office visit. As they headed to the truck, neither of them spoke.

Finally, once the baby was belted in the car seat and they drove toward the office, where Dani had left her car, Clay made the offer that had been simmering in his mind from the moment they left Guadalajara.

"I want you to come and stay at my ranch."

"Excuse me?" she asked, eyes wide, brow furrowed.

"I want you to take care of the baby for a while. Until I can find someone else."

"Are you out of your mind? I'm an attorney, not a nanny."

"I'll pay your usual fees."

By now, her voice had gone up several octaves. "You'd pay two-hundred and fifty dollars an hour for me to stay at your house and…and…*babysit?*"

It sounded a bit absurd, even to him. But he hadn't had time to find someone else yet, and Dani did great with the baby. Much better than he'd ever be able to do. He wasn't about to let her get away until Angela was happy and on the road to health. "I'm not asking you to take on a permanent position. I just need help until I can find someone else."

"Someone else?" she asked, her expression and tone clearly amazed. Or appalled. He wasn't quite sure what was going through her mind. "You're the one she needs to bond with, Clay."

"Yeah, but I'm not comfortable holding her. You know that." And he didn't do diapers, either. But he supposed that was a given.

"So force yourself to hold her, anyway," Dani said. "You'll get used to her before you know it."

"But what if I don't? What if I do something wrong and make her condition worse?"

The fact that Dani seemed to be gnawing on that possibility bothered him more than it should have. Hell, the longer she stayed quiet, the more he realized she was computing the probability that he *would* screw up—and with a kid who was already unhealthy.

"What do you say?" he asked.

Dani didn't know what to say. His offer was amazing. And ludicrous. No career woman in her right mind would consider it.

She glanced into the small, compressed back seat at the baby.

Clay did have a point. Angela had started to focus on Dani, to follow her with her eyes. Not a lot, mind you, just brief moments where it seemed as though that's what she was doing. Moments that were both exciting and scary.

Dani was glad that she might have played a role in putting a little spark in Angela's eyes. But the chance for upward mobility with the firm required her to be committed to her job, to the case she'd been working on before Clay stepped in and insisted she fly to Mexico.

Even if Martin was gung ho on the idea—after all, the firm would be racking up the hours in a situation like this—Dani was struggling to raise her younger brother and sisters. Clay was asking too much. She had her hands full trying to balance career and family as it was.

What was she supposed to tell Sara and the kids? Guess what, I'm going to move in with a client? And what about the trouble she would have finding a sitter for more than an overnight situation? She'd have to drag the kids along, too, taking them to the ranch.

Clay wasn't thinking clearly.

Looking after Angela was impossible. Dani couldn't agree to an offer like that. All she wanted to do was keep her brother and sisters on the straight and narrow, maintain her sanity until the children became self-sufficient and secure her position in the law firm. Of course, Martin might expect her to keep one of their top clients happy, especially since Clay wasn't balking at paying his nanny $250 an hour. The stubborn cattleman must be crazy. Or scared to death of the tiny girl.

"What are you proposing I do?" Dani asked. "Move out of my house, stay at your ranch and watch her until you find a suitable sitter?"

"Yeah. And maybe help me weed through the nanny applicants. I don't want to take any chances by hiring the first person who knocks on the door."

As much as she didn't like the idea of moving to the ranch, it wasn't a bad idea. Clay needed to bond with Angela, and in order for that to happen, he needed to be around her. Even though he might be paying Dani, she wouldn't let him get away with avoiding the child.

Dani looked at Angela. Poor little thing. She'd never asked for any of this: to be orphaned by the time she was two days old; to be left with an unbalanced caregiver who neglected her; or to be adopted by a grandfather who was afraid to touch her. She wanted to claim that her dog wasn't in this fight, but her heart went out to the infant.

"Okay," she said. "But there's a condition."

"What's that?"

"I can't possibly find a competent sitter for the kids who would be able to stay with them for an indefinite period of time. Even if I could, you got a glimpse of what Sara would put me through, not to mention the fact that Marcos and Delia need me. I may be stressed about trying to juggle family and career, but that doesn't mean I don't love those kids. Or that they don't love and need me."

"So what's the condition?"

"They'll have to stay at the ranch with me." She was prepared for him to balk, to complain, to tell her no.

Instead he said, "All right. How long will it take you to pack?"

"I have to discuss this with the kids first." She wasn't sure what kind of reaction she'd get out of any of them. Perhaps she could call it a family vacation.

"So go home and tell them."

"I also have to run this by Martin," she added.

"I'll handle him."

Dani had no doubt about that. From what she'd seen so far, Clay Callaghan was a man who didn't take no for an answer. When he wanted something, he went after it.

If she agreed to Clay's plan, the two of them would undoubtedly butt heads over the next few days, but she was up for it.

Of course, the fact that he'd seen her at her worst didn't exactly boost her confidence. Nor did the memory of the kiss they'd shared, now that she was thinking about moving into his house, where they'd pass each other in the hall. Eat at the same table.

She stole a glance at him, saw him watching her with an intensity that made it hard to breathe, to think. He reached across the seat and took her hand. The roughness of his callused palm and fingers stimulated her skin and sent a whisper of heat up her arm.

"I need you, Dani."

Oh, boy. He was talking about the baby. She knew that. But for a moment she could almost imagine him meaning that in another way. In a hungry way.

And she didn't mean dinner.

This was all about the baby, she reminded herself. This wasn't a sexual come-on, nor did she want it to be. So why the heated attraction? The crazy, girlish imaginings?

She tried to conjure a platonic expression. "Okay. For a few days. Just long enough for you to hire someone else."

His eyes locked on hers, and a smile spread across his face, turning her tummy inside out. "You won't regret this."

She already did. She felt as though she'd somehow sold out—even at the rate he agreed to pay. She was an attorney, for goodness sake, not a nanny. But he was right; the baby needed her. At least for the next couple of days.

Clay Callaghan might be forceful and determined, but she was, too. She'd make sure he bonded with that child, whether he liked it or not. Then she'd pack up the kids and take them home, leaving Clay to raise his granddaughter.

It would be a walk in the park, she told herself.

But when the cattleman gave her hand a squeeze, setting off a flurry of butterflies deep in her feminine core, she wasn't so sure about anything anymore. Not her ability to keep things professional. Not her ability to persuade him one way or another.

She didn't like the idea of being so darned attracted to a client. Especially when she already knew his kiss had the power to turn her knees—and her better judgment—to mush.

Chapter Seven

Once they reached the law firm building, Clay parked next to Dani's white Honda Civic, the only car left in the lot.

A couple of outdoor lights filled the interior of the truck with a silvery glow.

"You never did tell me how long it would take for you to pack," he said as Dani reached for the door handle.

"Surely you're not expecting me to come to the ranch this evening?"

Of course he was. This all had come down so fast—the priest's call, the decision to get the baby out of Mexico at any cost—that Clay hadn't given much thought to what he'd do with an infant once he brought her home.

He glanced in the back seat at the baby. "Who's going to take care of her tonight?"

"You are," she said.

"But what if she needs her diaper changed?"

"I'm sure she'll need it changed many times before the kids and I arrive tomorrow afternoon."

That's what he was afraid of. That and not knowing what to do if she cried. He shot a pleading look across the seat at the attractive attorney who'd gone to Mexico and back with him. "Aw, come on, Dani. You've been a real trooper so far. Don't leave me in a lurch now."

"You don't understand," she said. "I promised to take the kids to the movies as soon as I got back in town."

"I can respect that. But I have a fifty-two-inch plasma screen. You can rent them a movie and make popcorn."

"It's not the same."

"I'll even throw in candy and all the soda pop they can drink."

"That's a bad idea." She turned toward him, arms crossed under her breasts, the soft swell peeking over the scooped neckline of her cream-colored knit top. "Marcos has this thing with sugar. He starts bouncing off the walls."

Great. By day Clay worked hard. And at night he

appreciated the peace and quiet of his home. What a trade-off this was going to be, even if the kids were grain-fed, bound with duct tape and tucked in bed once the sun went down.

"Okay," he said. "Forget the sweet stuff. Does popcorn do anything to them?"

She merely studied him in the muted light. "Why are you doing this?"

"Doing what?"

"Wheeling and dealing. Trying to get me to see things your way. I'm actually looking out for your best interests, Clay."

"How is that?"

"I don't think you have any idea what will happen when my three siblings invade your ranch and rock your world."

She had a point, he supposed. But there was no way he was going to risk doing something wrong with Trevor's baby.

"Keep in mind, this isn't a permanent fix," she added. "It's strictly temporary until you can find someone else to help."

"I realize that."

"You'll have three extra kids to contend with."

To say that the added commotion wasn't a bit daunting was an understatement, but there was no way around it. He'd have to do his best to deal with it. "I've got a ranch to run, so I'll be outside all day."

"What about in the evening?" she asked.

That could be a problem, but he had a solution. "I'll lock myself in my room."

"All out of fear of the baby?"

"Angela has needs I can't even imagine."

"I can't believe this, Clay. You're as bad as Sara. You have an argument for everything." She tucked a strand of hair behind her ear, revealing a pair of pearl earrings and a neck meant for nuzzling. "I haven't even talked to Martin yet."

"That's another easy fix." Clay whipped out his cell and dialed the senior partner at home.

After a couple of rings, Martin's wife answered and told him she'd be happy to get her husband.

"You memorized Martin's telephone number?" Dani asked in a whispered tone that registered complete surprise. "Do you make a habit of calling him at home whenever you get a whim?"

"I pay top dollar for my whims, and Martin hasn't squawked about getting a call from me at his house in years."

She rolled her eyes, which he found strangely appealing. Most women didn't argue with him. Of course, he didn't keep them around very long if they did. But Dani was different. Rather than tall, blond and agreeable, she was short, brunette and spunky. If truth be told, he actually enjoyed sparring with her and knowing that he'd lit a spark of fire in her eyes.

Still, bottom line, the baby needed her. So that meant Clay needed her. But he wouldn't let Martin know she had become a maternal whiz because she had a flock of her own that might distract her at work.

When Martin answered, Clay explained his dilemma. "And since Ms. de la Cruz and I have sort of become a team when it comes to handling this baby, I want her to help me until I can hire someone who is far better at this stuff than either of us, which means I'm willing to pay her the usual hourly rate."

Ka-ching. Just as Clay knew he would, Martin jumped at the offer.

Clay gave Dani a single thumbs-up and winked.

On the outside, she seemed a bit annoyed, but her lips quirked in an interesting little grin, suggesting she had something up her sleeve.

As Clay proceeded to cut the call short, Dani reached across the seat and grabbed his forearm, her fingers gripping his flesh and setting off a shiver of heat through his blood. "I need to talk to him."

"Ms. de la Cruz wants to speak to you," Clay said, handing the phone to Dani.

The two discussed a project she'd been working on—a civil suit—and she asked Martin not to replace her. "I'll be able to work from the ranch on my laptop. I can also come into the office for a couple of hours a day."

No way, Clay thought. Dani seemed to think he'd get used to taking care of the baby, but that wasn't likely.

When the call ended, she crossed her arms and shook her head. "You're something else, Clay, I swear. You should have gone to law school. You make a formidable opponent when you set your mind to something."

He shrugged. "I'm used to getting what I want."

"So am I." She climbed from the truck.

"Wait a minute," he said. "You're going to need directions to the ranch."

"I know where it is. When I first went to work at the firm, I did some background work on their top clients. You were one of them." She reached for her purse, which sat on the seat, then paused. "By the way, thank you for not telling Martin about the kids."

"I might be a lot of things. Demanding and set in my ways comes to mind. But I'm a man of my word. I promised not to." He didn't mention when they'd struck that bargain—after they'd kissed and when he'd been tempted to take as much as she'd give. He didn't figure he needed to.

Her thoughts must have drifted in that same direction, because something fluttered between them, something that was charged and damn near alive.

Something they didn't dare pursue.

She tore her gaze away first, and he watched as she closed the passenger door and then dug through her purse. He waited until she climbed into her car, started the engine and headed out of the parking lot. As he threw his truck into gear and proceeded to drive back to the ranch, he had second thoughts about waiting for her to show up.

What if she changed her mind?

What if the kids whined and cried about missing the movie she'd promised them?

What if he was left alone with the baby?

Nope, he decided, as he pulled into the street and headed in the same direction she'd gone. He couldn't let that happen.

Dani might not like it, but he was going to follow her home and make sure she came to the ranch…tonight.

Dani pulled into the driveway and shut off the engine. As she got out of the car and locked it, a black dual-wheeled Chevy pickup parked along the curb.

Clay?

What was he doing here?

He climbed out of his truck and scanned the darkened front yard, where Marcos had left his red bicycle lying on its side in the middle of a lawn that needed to be mowed and next to a baseball bat and mitt.

She was torn between picking up the boy's clutter and asking Clay why he'd followed her home. But while taking care of Marcos' mess might make her feel less embarrassed, it wouldn't teach her brother anything. So she waited for Clay to speak.

He opened the passenger door, then appeared to study the car seat for a moment before calling out to her. "Hey. How do I get this thing disconnected?"

If anything, his inability to figure out the workings of an infant seat merely convinced her that he really was at a loss when it came to taking care of Angela.

She strode toward him, then pushed the red button that released the chair portion so he could carry Angela into the house without waking her.

"Why did you follow me home?" she asked.

"I thought you might want some backup with Sara."

He was probably right, but she didn't say anything. Instead they walked toward the porch.

The house was dark—except for the blue tint made by the television, which cast a haunted glow on the torn screen that was supposed to be on the front window but was now resting on top of a shrub. Near the welcome mat, a pair of inline skates—Delia's, Dani suspected—had been thoughtlessly discarded and left on the porch.

"Watch out," she said, pointing to the safety hazard, then stooping to move them aside.

"You'd better have a talk with those kids," he said. "Looks like a lawsuit ready to happen."

"That's why I decided to become an attorney. It was the most cost-efficient way to represent the legal interests of my family." She clucked her tongue. "So, welcome to my world."

She opened the door and let him into the house, only to step into an empty and darkened living room, the only sound and light coming from a television tuned to the Cartoon Network.

"Mrs. Fuentes?" Dani called.

"Yes, here I am," the woman answered, as she entered the room wiping her hands on her apron.

Dani introduced her to Clay, apologized about Sara's disappearance earlier that day, thanked her for helping out and then paid for her services. "Where are the kids?"

"In the kitchen. They're having ice cream for dessert, and I was just finishing up the dishes."

After Mrs. Fuentes gathered her things and left, Dani called the kids into the living room and turned on a couple of lamps. They seemed more surprised to see Clay than to have her home earlier than expected. She introduced her client to the children, then announced she had something to tell them.

"Is that a real live baby?" Delia asked, plopping down on her knees and peering at the carrier Clay had set on the floor near the sofa.

"Yeah," Clay said. "Her name's Angela."

"Oh, she's so cute." Delia, the sides of her long, curly hair pulled back with red barrettes, studied the infant in awe. "She's so tiny."

One down, two to go, Dani suspected. Then she glanced at Marcos and Sara, who lobbed Wimbledon-style gazes from Dani to Clay and back again.

"I have good news and bad news," Dani said.

"You're leaving again?" Sara asked, clearly not pleased.

Dani cleared her throat, then crossed her arms and shifted her weight to one foot, bracing herself for their reactions and hoping to sidestep potential problems by putting a spin on the situation. "We're going to get a family vacation this summer after all."

"Cool," Marcos said, eyes lighting up. "Where are we going?"

"Mr. Callaghan has invited us to stay on his ranch for a few days." She scanned their faces, looking for signs of disappointment and not seeing any—not even in Sara's expression, which bordered on surprise and disbelief.

"Do you have horses?" Sara asked Clay.

"It's a cattle ranch, but I have horses, too."

"Do you have any that we can ride?" the teen asked, her eyes growing wide.

"That can probably be arranged."

"Awesome," Sara said. "When are we going?"

"I figured you might want to go tonight," Clay said, completely taking over. "That way you can go for an early-morning ride. What do you think?"

"All right," the teen said. "Then I'd better go pack."

"Me, too!" Marcos said, as he took off on his sister's heels.

Delia continued to focus on the baby. "Can I hold her when she wakes up?"

"If it's okay with Dani," Clay said.

"Why does it have to be okay with her?" the little girl said. "It's your baby."

Clay didn't respond, which didn't surprise Dani. Even a child had figured out who should be in charge of the baby.

"Well," she said. "I guess I'd better throw some things together, too."

Twenty minutes later the kids piled into the car, happy and chattering about the unexpected vacation. But Dani knew better than to expect any rest and relaxation. Clay wasn't used to babies. That was a given. But just wait until the de la Cruz kids descended upon the ranch. She could see it all now.

Two-hundred-and-fifty dollars an hour didn't seem like nearly enough. She should have pushed for more.

Dani followed behind Clay's truck as he led them out of town and to the ranch that sprawled across the countryside and would have undoubtedly been more impressive had they arrived during the day.

Even though the kids had packed in a hurry, it was nearly bedtime when they arrived at the house, a three-story structure that Dani could only describe as an estate.

Sara carefully eyed the barn, the outbuildings and

a corral of horses. She didn't offer an opinion, but since she never held back a complaint, at least not lately, Dani considered her silence a positive response.

Clay parked near the barn, and Dani pulled up beside him. As they exited their vehicles, two black-and-white Australian shepherds greeted them, barking heartily and wagging their stubby tails.

"Cool," Marcos said, dropping to his knees to pet the dogs. "What are their names?"

"Mutt and Jeff," Clay told him, as he opened the door to get Angela, who was now awake.

This time he managed to get the baby's seat disengaged without help, which Dani chalked up as proof that he'd be able to handle things on his own soon, and her life could go back to normal.

"This one is kind of fat," Marcos said about the smaller of the two dogs. "He must like to eat."

"That's Mutt," Clay told him. "She's going to have a litter of pups in a couple of days."

"Wow," the boy said. "If you have any leftover puppies you don't have homes for, I'd like to have one."

"It's up to your sister," Clay said.

Marcos zapped Dani with pleading eyes. "Pleeease. I'd take super-good care of it."

"Aren't you the boy who left his bike and baseball gear in the front yard?" she asked.

"Yeah, but that's different."

As they headed to the house, which looked as though it had been built for a multigenerational family, rather than a single man who'd just lost his only son, a cowboy came out of one of the outbuildings. He wore an old felt hat, faded denim jeans and a pair of scuffed boots. He made his way toward them as though he'd just ridden in from the range, and Dani noticed a hitch in his gait.

"I thought you were just going after one kid," the cowboy said to Clay in a slow, Texas drawl. "But you came back with a whole passel of 'em."

"They were part of a package deal with the best and most expensive nanny I could find," Clay said. "Daniela de la Cruz, this is my foreman, Marvin Hawkins. Hawk, this is my attorney, as well as my temporary sitter."

The foreman reached out his arm to greet her, shaking her hand with a firm grip. Hawk, a weathered but pleasant-looking man she guessed to be in his mid-forties, tipped his hat slightly. "Pleased to meet you, ma'am."

"Same here." Dani offered him an olive-branch smile. "I'm afraid we're going to be staying at the ranch for a couple of days, so I hope you don't mind having kids around."

"Here, let me get that for you." Hawk took the overnight bag she carried. "As for kids, I don't have any of my own, but I've got a niece and nephew down in Galveston, so they broke me in pretty good."

As they neared the front porch, Hawk looked at the infant in the carrier Clay held by the handle like a picnic basket and blew out a whistle. "Dang, she's a tiny little thing."

"Yeah," Clay said to his foreman. "But we're working on that."

"How'd everything go in Mexico?" the foreman asked his boss.

"Not bad. Thanks to my attorney, I didn't end up in jail."

"That's good to know." Hawk grinned at Dani. "It was my idea to call you folks at the law office. Clay was hell-bent on going down there and bringing that baby home all by himself."

As the men shepherded the kids to the door, Dani noticed Hawk had more than a limp. He seriously favored his right leg. She wondered how he'd gotten hurt, whether it was a new injury or not. She wouldn't dare ask, though.

They entered a wide foyer with hardwood floors, and Clay led them to a huge family room with white plaster walls, dark wood beams and a stone fireplace. Brightly colored southwestern artwork added an interesting, Native American touch. Several brown leather sofas, expensive no doubt, provided a place to sit and enjoy the plasma television he'd told her about. The scent of lemon oil, as well as an absence of clutter, suggested Clay hired household help, since Dani couldn't imagine the rugged rancher being responsible for the polished hardwood floors and the dust-free furniture.

"You obviously have a housekeeper," Dani said. "Why don't you ask her to watch the baby?"

"She only comes in a couple of times a week. Besides, she's not into kids."

What was that supposed to mean? Dani wanted to ask, but decided to let it ride until the kids turned in for the night.

"Are there any rules we should be aware of?" Dani asked.

"For the most part, they can have the run of the place—other than my study, which is off-limits." Clay made a point of looking each child in the eye. "Just don't give me reason to change the rules, and we'll be fine."

"Where's your study?" Delia asked. "I don't want to go in there on accident."

Clay grinned. "It's upstairs, the second door on the left."

The little girl smiled. "I just won't go upstairs, okay? Sometimes I get left and right mixed up."

Clay gave one of her braids a gentle tug. "That's where your bedroom is going to be. So I'll point it out when we get there, okay?"

She nodded.

"Come on," he said. "I'll show you to your rooms."

As Clay led them upstairs and down the hall, he

stopped at the first bedroom and offered it to Marcos. The next two were assigned to the girls. And the last, which was next to the prohibited study, went to Dani.

Each room was neat, yet she couldn't help noticing the furnishings were sparse. There were no pictures on the walls, no homey touches. But then again Clay probably didn't have need of guest rooms very often.

The kids each staked their claims and left their bags in the room they'd been assigned. Quickly settling in, she supposed. Dani opted to do that later, once she'd gotten Angela ready for bed.

She wondered where Clay's room was located, what it looked like, what kind of furniture he had. Whether it was more lived in than the rest of the house, but she scolded herself for being curious.

Before she could follow the kids downstairs, Clay stopped her. "You, by the way, have permission to use the study."

For a heart-pounding moment their gazes locked and something buzzed between them. An intimacy, she supposed. A bond they'd formed on the plane and in Mexico. The kiss they'd shared.

She'd be darned if she knew what to do with it, so she broke the invisible connection and headed downstairs.

When they returned to the family room, Marcos pointed to the large plasma television mounted on the wall. "Hey. Look at that. It's just like having a private movie theater."

"Hawk," Clay said to the foreman who was sitting on the sofa. "Why don't you show them how that thing works and find them something to watch. I'll see if Dani needs anything for the baby."

Within moments, the kids had each taken a seat on the sofa and watched as Hawk surfed the channels.

"Can I get you anything?" Clay asked Dani.

"How about a towel and Angela's diaper bag. I'd like to bathe her and get her ready for bed."

"Sure. But speaking of beds…" His brow furrowed. "I don't have one for her, but I'll get one tomorrow. For tonight, I guess we'll just have to make do."

"That's easy enough," Dani said, removing the baby from the carrier and picking up the diaper bag. "I'll figure out something."

"Do you want me to show you a bathroom that has a tub?" he asked.

"That's all right. Just take me to the kitchen. I'll bathe her in the sink."

For some reason, Dani expected Clay to let her tend Angela alone, but he hung out with her during the bath and a shampoo the baby didn't like.

"She's crying," Clay said, as though Dani couldn't hear.

"I don't think she's been bathed very often, so this is all new to her."

"Yeah, well, I don't like it when she cries." The tension in his angular jaw, the uneasiness in his rugged features confirmed his words.

"She'll get used to having her hair shampooed," Dani said. "And you'll get used to hearing her fuss."

"I doubt it."

While Angela lay on a soft stack of folded white towels placed on the countertop, Dani dressed her in a lavender sleeper, then bundled her in a receiving blanket. All the while Clay watched her every move.

"Why don't you fix her bottle," Dani said, realizing that was another job Clay would have to take over soon.

She had to talk him through it, but he managed to prepare six ounces and warm it. As Dani settled into one of the kitchen chairs to feed the baby, Clay took one, too. Just watching. But not like a student observing a tutor. There was a mama-bear look in his eyes.

Clay might not feel comfortable handling the baby, but that didn't mean he wasn't going to insist that whatever nanny he hired treat her well. A good thing, Dani decided. The little girl deserved to be loved and cared for.

Dani watched the baby in her arms. "You know, she seems to be eating better."

"Oh, yeah? Good."

They sat like that awhile, quiet and still.

"I'll have Hawk take the kids horseback riding to-morrow," Clay said, "if that's all right with you. They may as well enjoy themselves while they're here, es-pecially since you told them it was their vacation."

"That would be nice. I'm sure they'll enjoy it. And while they're gone, I'll take the baby into town and find a suitable crib."

"All right. I'll give you a credit card to use. Feel free to pick up anything else we're going to need."

Silence again, this time more awkward than the last.

Was it the sense of teamwork? A common goal that bound them together, connecting them when they were both better off on their own?

"Hawk seems like a nice guy," Dani said, hoping to change the subject and lift the silence. "How long has he worked for you?"

"A couple of years. He used to work for a rancher outside of San Antonio, but was in a bad car accident and nearly lost his right leg. His boss let him go, and I hired him. I suspect Tom Bowman, the other rancher, thought Hawk was damaged goods."

"But you didn't?" she asked.

"Hawk's got one hell of a head for cattle. For all animals, actually. Besides, he's loyal and honest."

She supposed Clay's admiration of the man shouldn't surprise her. But in a way it did, because it proved he had a compassionate, thoughtful side to him.

Dani removed the nearly empty bottle from the sleeping baby's mouth, lifted Angela carefully and burped her. "I think it's time to put her to bed. Can you please help me?"

"Sure. What do you want me to do?"

"Well, it might be easier if she sleeps with me tonight. So, if you'll push my bed against the wall so she can't fall off, that would help."

Clay got to his feet, led her upstairs and down the hall to the room she was to use then moved the queen-size bed with little effort.

"Can I get you to pull the blankets back?" she asked.

When he did, she laid the baby in bed, stretching to place her on the side closest to the wall. For some reason, Clay remained close, and as Dani drew back and stood upright, her arm brushed against him, against the heat of his body. He was tall and muscular, a mountain of a man who didn't appear to let anything wear him down. And the fact that a defenseless baby scared the liver out of him was… She didn't know. Kind of amusing, she supposed.

His scent, musky and unique with a hint of cowboy, settled over her, as did that attraction that was becoming all too familiar. Their gazes locked, and something swirled around them. Something awkward yet stirring. Something that had nothing to do with babies or law firms or ranches and everything to do with that kiss they'd shared in Guadalajara.

She wasn't sure how she knew that the knee-buckling memory was taunting them both, but she did. And she sensed it was about to happen again.

Her game plan had been to act as if the kiss hadn't happened. But for some reason pretending wasn't working right now.

All she had to do was take a step forward, slip her arms around his neck. Make the first move.

But she couldn't.

She *wouldn't*.

Because tonight she couldn't blame the alcohol for a lapse of good sense.

Just forget it, she told herself.

But ignoring that kiss wasn't working, either, and since they would be living in the same house for a couple of days, they were going to have to get past it.

"I, uh…" She cleared her throat. "I'm sorry about what happened last night."

"Are you talking about the kiss?"

She nodded. "It was unprofessional of me. I just wanted to get it out in the open so that we could quit tripping over it."

"Don't worry," he said, taking a step back. "It's forgotten."

But as he left the room, she realized that memory was just as real as ever. Just as alive. Because even though Clay had walked away, the desire to kiss him again hadn't left with him.

Chapter Eight

Just before daybreak Clay gave up the fight for a good night's sleep, kicked off the covers and jumped in the shower.

A hot, pounding spray of water kneaded the tight muscles in his neck and back, refreshing him in a way his bed hadn't. Then he dried off, shaved, threw on his clothes and headed for the kitchen, where Mutt slept on a pad near the stove.

The Australian shepherd female had been his son's dog. Four years ago Trevor had picked her out as a pup because she'd been the runt of the litter. The boy had actually become teary-eyed when he had to leave her behind and go to college.

Wasn't it great?

Trevor had felt worse about leaving his dog behind than he had the ranch.

Or his dad.

But whose fault was that? Not the dog's.

Since her pups were due anytime, Clay brought her in the house at night. He liked having her close so he could keep an eye on her. She was still smaller than average, and he hoped she wouldn't have any problems.

"Hey, girl." He bent and gave her ears a rub. "How're you feeling, huh?"

Mutt yawned, apparently hanging in there.

"It shouldn't be too much longer." A day or so, Clay suspected.

He straightened, then put on a pot of coffee. As the brew gurgled and sputtered, he walked out to the service porch and glanced out the window. It was going to be a nice day. And a long one, he suspected.

Right now, the house and the ranch were just the way he liked it. Quiet and peaceful. But that wouldn't last long. Sooner or later everyone would wake up.

He'd like to blame his tossing and turning on having a houseful of people. But it wasn't the kids or the baby who had his mind too tangled to sleep. It was Dani and what he'd had the urge to do last night.

When they'd put the baby to bed, he'd been

sorely tempted to take her in his arms, to kiss her senseless the way he'd done just twenty-four hours before in Guadalajara.

But what would that have gotten them?

Nothing but trouble.

He needed Dani. And he wasn't about to complicate matters by letting sexual urges get the better of him.

There were a hundred reasons why he shouldn't pursue that kind of a relationship with her—and her age was one. She was too damn young for a man who'd mellowed over the years and become a loner. She probably enjoyed going out in the evenings, clubbing and the like.

Of course, he'd done a little socializing when he was her age—and younger. But hanging out at honky-tonks had been more his style.

A baby's cry, soft and more like a fuss, sounded.

He suspected Dani would be getting up and fixing Angela a bottle. As he stood at the back door, the sun was just beginning to rise, so he decided to talk to Hawk about the work that needed to be done that day. But as he reached for the doorknob, a vision came to him. Dani trying to juggle the baby in her arms while opening up a can of formula, pouring it in the bottle and screwing on a nipple.

Hell, he'd seen how she'd done it. The least he could do was make it easier for her. So instead of going outside as planned, he prepared the bottle, then held it under the hot water in the sink to warm it up a bit.

The sound of the baby's cry grew louder, and as Dani entered the kitchen, their eyes met. She wore a blue robe over a white cotton gown, and her hair was rumpled from sleep. When she was dressed in a business suit, she was attractive, but seeing her like that, fresh out of bed, was…

Damn.

Seeing her first thing in the morning was just plain arousing.

He shut off the faucet, then handed her the bottle. "I figured you'd be needing this."

"Thank you."

He studied her for a while, watched as she balanced the baby in her arms and offered the warmed formula. Watched the lapel of the robe slip aside, revealing the plain but sexy strip of a white cotton nightgown against her tanned skin. Not much, just enough to tweak his interest more than was comfortable.

Damn.

He cleared his throat, then pulled out a chair for her. "Have a seat."

"Thank you."

His only response was a nod, yet he watched a moment longer as her gaze met the baby's. Then he tore himself away.

"I'll see you later," he said, as he stepped toward the

back porch. "I need to talk to Hawk and the ranch hands." Then he called for Mutt, hightailed it out of the kitchen and walked outside, taking the dog with him.

Later that morning, after he and Hawk had lined out the other men—those who stayed on the ranch and those who drove in from town—he returned to the kitchen. There he found Dani frying bacon and eggs for the kids who were all seated at the table, with little Angela nestled in her carrier like a centerpiece.

But his gaze, as well as his interest, drifted back to Dani. She'd showered and dressed in a black T-shirt and a pair of faded blue jeans. Her feet, with red polish on the toes, were bare.

"Are you hungry?" she asked.

Yeah. But it was a different hunger she stirred standing there like that. Like she belonged in his kitchen. In his house. Maybe even in his life, albeit temporarily.

Damn again.

The aroma of fresh-brewed coffee—she'd made a new pot—and sizzling bacon mingled together, snaking around his gut and snagging him in a way that made him want to bolt. So even though he was hungry, he politely declined and slipped outside without striking up much of a conversation with anyone.

He was met by Mutt and Jeff, cropped tails wagging. They were eager to get to work and get their lives back on track.

So was Clay.

Having all those kids around was going to be different—and trying, he supposed. Of course, that was another reason to steer clear of anything remotely sexual with Dani—assuming she'd even be willing. Because if he entered into any kind of romantic relationship with her, he'd have to deal with her sisters and brother at least on occasion.

Not that they were ornery kids. Hell, even Sara, who obviously could be a handful when she put her mind to it, hadn't proved to be too much trouble. Yet. But Clay was used to coming and going as he pleased, to having things quiet at night. To walking around the house in the raw if he felt like it. And the kids put a damper on that. In fact, he wasn't sure how he was going to handle having them underfoot for the next several days.

He drove the truck out on the county road and down a piece, to the stretch of grazing land that bordered Emmett Keller's place, where he'd sent a couple of men to mend the fence earlier this morning. He checked their progress, then pointed out a few other sections he'd been concerned about.

When he returned home, he spotted Hawk giving Marcos and Sara riding tips and helping them saddle two old mares that wouldn't give inexperienced riders any trouble. Clay watched them from a distance, yet was close enough to hear them speak.

"Have either of you ridden a horse before?" Hawk asked the youngsters.

"I have," Sara said. "When my dad was still alive, he took me to the stables a couple of times. And Jessica, my friend, has her very own horse that she boards at an equestrian place. Once, when I didn't have to babysit, I went with her, and she let me ride her palomino."

"Hey, Mr. Callaghan," Marcos called to Clay from his mount. "Aren't you coming with us?"

The boy's eyes, bright and enthusiastic, struck a soft spot in Clay. But not in a way that made him feel like joining in the fun. Instead Marcos stirred up memories Clay had hoped to forget. Memories of the times he'd taken Trevor riding fences. Outings that had been forced in hopes that the city boy would gain an appreciation for the ranch. But Trevor hadn't been impressed. And the more Clay tried, the more withdrawn the boy had become.

"I'm afraid not," Clay told Marcos. "I can't go with you this time. I've got some office work to do."

Before Clay got two steps toward the house, Sara and Marcos laughed at something Hawk said, reinforcing the fact that the foreman had a knack with kids and was much better suited for supervising the riding lessons than Clay. But that was okay. Hawk was good people.

The two men didn't talk much about the past, but from what Clay had gathered, Hawk and his late wife hadn't been able to have children, which was too bad. Unlike Clay, Hawk would have made a good father.

As Clay neared the front porch, Dani and Delia came out the door. They had Angela all dolled up in a bright-yellow outfit with a little flowery doodad in her dark hair—an added feminine touch he would have never considered.

How the hell did he expect to raise that poor baby girl?

He didn't. Not without full-time help.

"Guess what," Delia said, her smile revealing a missing front tooth. Had it been there last night? He hadn't noticed.

"What's that?" Clay asked.

"We're going to the mall. The first thing we're going to buy is a stroller, and when we do, I get to push it."

"Your sister is lucky to have you as a helper." Clay shot a glance at Dani, saw her dressed casually in the same pair of snug jeans that molded to her hips, plus a white blouse with the top couple of buttons undone. She wore her hair, silky black strands that glistened in the morning light, curled under at the shoulders.

As she strode toward the car, the sun's rays gave her a healthy glow, an attractive aura.

"Did you want to go with us?" Dani asked him.

He didn't know what made him more uneasy.

Shopping, which he didn't much care for anyway, or spending the day with Dani, which shouldn't be the least bit tempting, yet was.

"Nope," he said. "I've got a ton of work to do. But have fun."

"We will." The wind whipped a strand of hair across her cheek, and she brushed it away. "How much do you want me to spend? This could get expensive."

He'd never been a tightwad. "Buy everything the baby will need. And have lunch on me, ladies."

Delia tossed him another gap-toothed grin, which in itself was enough to soften his heart. But the appreciative smile Dani flashed him made his chest swell and his pulse thump like a son of a gun.

What a mess he'd jumped into.

All he'd wanted was to finally do right by Trevor, which meant opening his home to an orphaned infant. But then he'd been forced to let the Brady Bunch move in.

As tough as it was for him to adjust, they seemed to be settling right in.

Just like one big, awkward family.

The shoppers didn't return until dusk, and when they arrived, the car was loaded down with bags and boxes. But Clay didn't see anything big enough to hold a baby's bed.

"Where's the crib?" he asked, as he came around to the trunk to help Dani remove her purchases.

It was Delia who answered. "The bed is coming in a little bit. We paid a man to bring it in his truck with all the other big stuff."

"Big stuff?" Clay asked Dani. "For a little baby?"

"A swing, a dresser for her clothes, a Pack-N-Play for her to use downstairs and that sort of thing. You didn't appear to be concerned about the cost, but I kept all the receipts."

"I don't care about the money."

She tossed him a smile. "That's good, because I didn't want to have to go back and return things tomorrow."

"We bought pizza, too," Delia announced. "Pepperoni and the kind Dani likes. Veggie. Yuck."

"It's still in the car," Dani said. "I'll cook tomorrow night. I'm too pooped to think about it now."

"Don't feel as though you have to be chief cook and bottle washer. I can handle kitchen duty."

She arched a brow as though she didn't believe him. Or as though she was afraid to eat what he might come up with. He hadn't taken cooking classes, but he knew how to grill perfect steaks. And what was so hard about baking potatoes or making a salad?

"Maybe we'll have a cook-off and let the kids decide," he said. He also knew how to make great homemade ice cream, which ought to sway the judges.

"I might have to take you up on that." She grinned, then nodded her pretty head toward the car. "Why don't you get dinner tonight. It's in the back seat."

Fifteen minutes later they'd all washed up and were seated at the kitchen table, paper plates loaded high with slices of pizza.

"Bluebonnet is the coolest horse," Sara said, while removing the slices of pepperoni from her pizza and stacking them to the side. "She's even better than Goldie, Jessica's palomino. Hawk said I can ride her every single day that we're here."

Clay poured himself a glass of iced tea from the pitcher he'd brewed earlier in the day. "There's a certain responsibility that goes along with having a horse. So if you're going to ride Bluebonnet, maybe you ought to be taking care of her, too."

"No problem." Sara reached for a napkin and wiped the pepperoni grease from her fingers. "We brushed the horses down when we got finished."

"Good. But I'm talking about mucking out her stall," Clay said. "And feeding her each day and making sure she has fresh water."

"Are you kidding?" Sara asked. "That would be so cool. I'd love to do all that for her. It would almost be like having a horse of my own."

Clay had expected the young teenager to balk, like Trevor had done when forced to do ranch chores, but instead the girl surprised him.

"Can I take care of Daisy Mae, too?" Marcos asked.

It appeared that he was two for two when it came to finding enthusiastic new ranch hands. "Sure. That's part of the deal."

"And maybe," the boy added, "if Dani sees how good I am with a horse, she'll let me have one of Mutt's puppies."

Clay's gaze met Dani's in an adult-style connection, a tenuous bond. He figured he'd better tread lightly. He wasn't sure how she felt about him putting the kids to work, but it seemed like the right thing to do. And not just because that's what Rex had insisted upon the first day Clay had come to stay at the ranch.

"Hey," Clay told the boy, "I have no problem giving you a puppy, but first it has to be okay with your sister. Then I need to be absolutely certain that you will be the one feeding it, taking it for walks, cleaning up the backyard and making it mind."

"I promise," the boy said. "I'll even shovel up poop every day. Just you wait and see. I never had to be responsible before."

Neither had Trevor. So when he'd moved in with Clay, he'd been given chores to do. He'd done what was asked of him, but it was obvious that he'd hated doing them. It had been a shame, too. Clay had hoped Trevor would be excited about the place he would have inherited one day.

While Sara and Marcos rambled on and on about

the horses, the riding lessons and the ranch, they also sang Hawk's praises. But Clay supposed that was to be expected.

After downing three slices of pizza and two glasses of iced tea, he excused himself and went into his study to make a couple of phone calls. He'd made an offer on some property up north through a limited liability company he was involved with and wanted to know if there'd been a counteroffer. One call led to another, and by the time he came out of the study, it was quiet in the house. Apparently, Hawk had worn out the older kids, and shopping had tired both the baby and Delia. Clay relished the silence, which convinced him everyone had turned in for the night—something he ought to do, as well.

As he headed to his room, a drip, drip, drip sounded through the open doorway of the guest bathroom. The plumbing was in good working order, so he suspected that one of the kids had neglected to completely shut off the faucet. He stepped inside, only to find the mirror still fogged.

The sink was fine. So then he looked at the tub, where a white lacy bra dangled from the curtain rod and reminded him that his house had been overrun with females. As he drew back the curtain, he found the leaking spigot and shut the faucet tight, only to have the brassiere fall into the tub.

Oops. He picked it up and studied it momentarily, wondering who it belonged to, who had washed it out and left it to dry. By the full cup size, he easily surmised it belonged to Dani. It was made of white satiny material and had a lace trim that snagged on his work-roughened hands, not that he was doing anything other than putting it back where it had been hanging. As he slipped it over the rod, he felt a pair of eyes on him.

Uh-oh. He didn't want anyone to think he was a pantie nabber. He turned to see Dani in the open doorway, her lips parted, her face flushed.

Clay gave Dani a taunting grin that sent a bevy of butterflies swarming in her chest and nearly buckled her knees. His gaze settled over her, warming the bathroom and causing the steam to rise, the walls to close in on her. On them.

She hadn't meant to leave her undies hanging about for anyone to see or stumble upon, but the baby had spit up on her earlier, and she hadn't wanted the formula to stain her new bra. She just assumed Clay had his own bathroom and had never expected him to come into this one.

"Is it in your way?" Dani asked. "I can put it someplace else to dry."

"Actually, it's fine where it is. When I tried to tighten the faucet, I accidentally knocked it down."

She thought of the delicate undergarment in his big hands and couldn't help thinking it was cute. No, *cute* wasn't the right word. There was something sexual about a man's hands on a bra. She could almost imagine Clay's hands on her. Touching. Seeking. Unsnapping the hook. Releasing her breasts.

Great. Weren't things bad enough between them without her imagination kicking it up a sexual notch?

Before either one of them could conjure a response, the baby cried out from the room down the hall.

"Hey, she's not going to roll out of bed," he asked, "is she?"

"While you were busy in the office, the delivery man came. He set up the crib for us. She's safe." Dani listened, caught another fussy sound. "I guess I'd better go to her and reassure her that everything's okay. She shouldn't be hungry again."

"It wouldn't hurt to offer her more milk," Clay said. "She has some catching up to do in the weight department."

That was true; although Angela had eaten just an hour or so ago. But Dani liked the idea that Clay was concerned about feeding her. And that he was willing to fix a bottle. It wasn't enough, but it was a start.

"Thanks, Clay. I appreciate your help."

As he headed for the kitchen, she went to the bedroom she'd decided to share with Angela, the room where she'd instructed the delivery man to set up the crib and dresser. A night-light cast a warm glow inside, allowing her to see the baby wasn't really awake.

She placed her hand lightly on the baby's tummy. "Shhh. It's okay, Angie. I'm here. Shhh."

Apparently, the sound of Dani's voice was enough to lull the baby back to sleep. So she tiptoed from the room and headed to the kitchen to tell Clay not to bother with the bottle. But when she entered, she spotted him through the doorway that led to the service porch. He was kneeling and petting the dog.

"What's the matter?"

He turned, a grin busting across his angular face and setting off a glimmer in his green eyes. "I'm sorry. Mutt's having puppies, and I got distracted."

Dani crept forward, not wanting to worry the new mother. "That's okay. Angela went back to sleep, so I came to tell you we didn't need a bottle after all."

Clay gently lifted a tiny ball of black-and-white fur and held it close to his cheek. "Look at this."

"How sweet." And she wasn't just talking about the puppy. Rather it was the man gently holding the newborn, the hint of boyish delight in his smile.

She eased closer, her eyes on the pup, her thoughts on the man. "You know, Clay. You're not at all uneasy about holding that little guy. But you're scared of Angela. Why is that?"

He returned the puppy to its mother. "I don't

know. I've grown up around animals. I know what they need, what they expect from me."

It sounded as if he thought that wasn't the case when it came to humans, and she wondered what had made him come to that conclusion.

She knelt beside him, petting Mutt and counting four pups besides the one Clay had been holding. "Well, you've certainly got a way with dogs."

He shrugged. "If you treat them right, and they know what to expect from you, dogs are loyal. They won't run off—even when you've had a bad day and take it out on them."

"Are we talking about how your dad ran off and left you?" she asked.

He tensed and leaned back. "Why do I get the idea that you had two majors in college—prelaw and psychology?"

"I'm sorry if I struck a tender chord."

They sat there for a while, close enough to touch yet maintaining a distance while watching the birth of another puppy.

"You know," Clay said. "Now that you brought it up, I just realized that my old man left when I wasn't much younger than Delia. I still can't believe a man could just get up one day, walk out the door, leave his family and drive off without ever looking back."

"There was your mom, too. In a way, she left you as well...from the cancer." Dani tucked a strand of hair behind her ear and rested her bottom on her heels. "We have quite a few things in common, I suppose."

"Oh, yeah?"

"Because my mom took off when I was so young, too. And that made losing my dad especially tough. I wasn't ready for him to die. Or to be left alone. I'd expected him to raise the kids so that I'd be able to focus on my career. And when the time came for me to have a child of my own, I wanted him to be a grandfather."

"But it didn't work out the way you expected." Clay placed a hand on her shoulder, a big hand. A warm hand. "Listen, Dani. In spite of your worries and insecurities, you're doing just fine with the kids. And Martin is happy to have you on-board at the firm."

Her worries? Her insecurities?

How did he know about that?

Aw, shoot. That must have been what she'd rambled on about when they'd flown to Guadalajara. Not just the fact that she was raising kids and her colleagues at the firm didn't know it. But that she was doing such a poor job of it, too.

"Rex had never been around kids," Clay said. "So I cut him some slack. He had his faults, but he did right by me. I tried to do the same thing with Trevor when he came to live with me on the ranch, and I did my best to help him become a man."

"You sent him off to college," Dani reminded him, "providing him with an education."

"Yeah, well college was his idea. Ranching was mine. But even after I tried to respect the differences between us, I couldn't seem to connect with him. Not like Rex had done with me."

"I'm sure you did all right. And that your son loved you."

"I guess." He raked a hand through his hair. "But we weren't exactly close. I'm thinking I might have been too hard on him."

She knew where he was going with that. He was afraid he'd hurt Angela one way or another, maybe by doing something wrong now that she was an infant. Or by being too tough on her as she grew up. That's what Dani would have to work on. *His* fears. *His* insecurities. "You're going to be a good father to Angela, Clay."

"You think so?"

She certainly hoped so. She couldn't hang out at the ranch forever. She needed to get back to the office—where she belonged.

"I know so." She cast him a warm, heartfelt smile that she was afraid promised more than she could deliver. "Think of her as a puppy, eager for your love and affection."

"Yeah, but these cute little guys grow up, pee on the floor, chew on everything in sight. Then it's time to clamp down on them." He reached out and gave her shoulder a gentle squeeze. "But thanks for the vote of confidence."

He released her, ending the tenderness they'd shared and making her heart ache for something she couldn't quite put her finger on.

Something he kept locked inside of himself.

Chapter Nine

Two days later, while Dani cleaned up the remnants of a hotcake breakfast, Clay lingered over a cup of coffee, then snagged a piece of sausage from the platter that was still on the table. Near the refrigerator, Angela sat in her new battery-operated swing, while it lulled her to sleep.

"How's the nanny hunt going?" Dani asked. "We're well into our 'vacation' on the ranch, and you've yet to interview one person for the job."

"I got a couple of calls yesterday," he said. "But the first woman didn't want to move this far out of town. And the other one isn't available until after she returns from a two-week Caribbean cruise that a previous employer paid for."

"At least her references ought to be good," Dani said. "But to tell you the truth, I'd rather not have to wait that long."

"I figured you'd say that." Clay strode toward the kitchen window and peered out into the southern sky. Dark clouds formed on the horizon. He didn't need to hear a weather report to know a storm was on the way.

As he turned to put his cup into the sink, the phone rang, and he answered on the second ring. "Hello?"

It was Brian Westlake, one of the attorneys at Dani's firm. He wanted to talk to her, so Clay handed her the receiver. "It's for you."

"Thanks."

"Hey," she said, lighting up at the sound of the guy's voice.

The fact that Brian could call out of the blue and lift her mood like that niggled at Clay in a way that made him uneasy. She'd told him before how much she liked her job, so he shouldn't give it another thought. But which attorney was Brian Westlake? Wasn't he the new man they'd hired? Thirtyish, six foot something, blond hair?

The guy with the dazzling smile?

As Clay realized that's exactly who Brian was, the niggling grew stronger until it blossomed into a full-blown, grinding knot.

The two attorneys talked for a while, and from

what Clay could gather, they were working on some case that had hit a standstill. He also sensed that Dani was chomping at the bit to get involved.

"You know," she told Brian, "I might be able to slip away for a while and come into the office this morning."

Clay didn't want her to leave. Not with a storm coming in, not when he would be locked inside a warm and dry house with all the kids.

When she glanced at him, he shook his head in a no-way-in-hell manner, letting her know he wasn't ready to handle the family stuff yet. Not today. So he whipped out the roll of cash he kept in his front pocket and flashed it at her, letting her know he was paying a stiff, hourly rate to retain her. *Here.*

"Hang on a minute," she told Brian, then she pressed her hand over the mouthpiece and whispered, "This is important, Clay. I really need to go into the office for a while. Your housekeeper is coming today. Surely, between the two of you—not to mention Sara and Delia—you can handle this."

Maybe he could. But he didn't like the idea. Not one bit. A cold sense of panic rushed through his veins, but she didn't seem to give a damn about it.

"I'll meet you at the office," she told Brian. "I can leave here in less than an hour."

Forty-three minutes later, much to Clay's chagrin, that's exactly what she did.

In spite of his reservations, the morning passed

without a major incident. Sara, who'd been a lot more agreeable lately—thanks in large part to Blue-bonnet, no doubt—promised to stay inside and help with Angela. Apparently, she'd been around babies in the past—Delia for one. So that gave Clay a little relief. And even Delia, who clutched a lifelike doll of her own, was happy to pitch in. She was only six, but she seemed to know the baby's schedule and never tired of running for diapers or talking to Angela, who, at times, seemed to track the little girl's movements.

But Barbara Grainger, the housekeeper who cleaned on Mondays and Fridays, failed to show up. At 10:30, Clay gave her a call on her cell phone, only to learn that she'd forgotten what day it was, had gone to the beauty salon and was resting her head over a shampoo bowl, her hair wet and lathered. She apologized, but a lot of good that did him now.

Barbara was a nice woman in her early forties, but she'd been in a car accident a few years back and had suffered a serious head injury, which had left her with memory lapses. She also had a bum shoulder that gave her trouble when it rained, which she reminded him about while they chatted.

"This one is going to be a gully washer," she said. "I can feel it coming."

He really ought to consider getting someone more reliable, but he had this thing about taking in strays. And he didn't need a shrink to tell him why.

When his mom was sick and couldn't work, the money she'd managed to save from her tips ran out and things were pretty bleak. Besides not having enough to eat, they'd also received an eviction notice. God only knew where the two of them would have ended up if Rex hadn't offered them a place to stay. The gruff and crotchety rancher who'd taken a liking to Clay's mom had provided room, board and hope.

So Clay was just paying it forward, he supposed. But dammit. Why did Barbara have to forget to come to the ranch today?

The phone rang, and when Clay picked it up, it was the real estate broker who'd been trying to put together the land deal he and his partners were involved in. Another parcel nearby might also be available at a decent price, and he wanted to know if Clay would be interested in driving out to see it.

"Not today," he told him.

In the background the children's voices grew steadily louder, although he hadn't heard a peep from the baby. So he continued to focus on the business at hand, trying his damnedest to shut out the squabble brewing in the background.

"Stop it."

"Don't."

"I didn't."

"Get away from the baby."

"That's mine."

"Give it back."

When Angela let out a shriek in protest, Clay decided to end the call and scold the whole lot of them. But before he could do so, Delia screamed and yelled, "Marcos, no! You're hurting her."

In a burst of pink, a flannel-wrapped infant flew across the room, and Clay's heart plunged to his gut. He dropped the telephone receiver to the floor with a clunk. A curse burst from his lips as he raced to the child.

It took a long, agonizing moment for Clay to realize it had been Delia's dolly that had been airborne and not the real baby. The sheer emotion that had built in his chest—the frustration, the fear, the guilt that always lurked—was overwhelming. He swore again, then sent Delia and Marcos to their rooms.

"For how long?" the boy asked.

"Right now, it's a life sentence with no chance of parole."

Marcos, remorse splashed across his face, dashed off without uttering another word.

But Delia's bottom lip quivered, and she blinked back a flood of tears. Then, with a wounded glance that sliced clear through Clay's chest, she retrieved the doll from the floor and trudged up the stairs.

Sara merely stared at him as though he'd gone mad, and he couldn't blame her. He'd completely lost it. He blew out a ragged breath, then raked his hand through his hair. That was it. He couldn't handle this one minute longer.

Dani had to come home.

Now.

In the past few days Dani had missed the hustle and bustle of the busy law firm, and it felt good to be back in the office and right in the thick of things.

There was a certain satisfaction in putting a case together and knowing that, barring any surprises, her client would win. But as she sat behind her polished cherrywood desk and pored over a brief she'd nearly finished writing, Brian Westlake entered her office.

At thirty-three, Brian was the latest addition to the firm. He was also a handsome man who'd made not-so-subtle hints that he'd like to pursue something with Dani on a personal level. To be honest, she welcomed his friendship, as well as the flirtation. His smile, his charm and his reputation in the legal community reminded her of the life she wanted for herself, the romance she dreamed of having with another professional and the social sphere she hoped would allow her to escape from all the family squabbles.

But Brian was dangling a carrot she shouldn't pursue.

Even if something romantic developed between them, the reality of Dani's world would dull the glow in no time at all. Still, that didn't mean she couldn't flirt back and pretend that things could develop between them. Did it?

Brian cleared his throat as he approached her desk. "I'm glad you're back. The office isn't the same without your smile."

"It isn't, huh?" The fact he'd missed her was nice. Flattering, to be honest.

"What's the deal with you and Callaghan?" he asked.

"Excuse me?"

"Martin says he's paying you the usual hourly rate to stay at his house and babysit. Has the old guy been smoking too much wacky tobaccy?"

"Absolutely not." She wanted to add, And he's *not* old. Instead she said, "His granddaughter has been neglected, and I...sort of bonded with her. So until he can hire a competent sitter, he needs my assistance."

Brian grinned. "Nannies aren't that hard to find. When my sister decided to go back to work, she contacted a referral service, and she had someone in less than thirty-six hours. Maybe Callaghan's just trying to put the moves on you."

"Don't be ridiculous," she said. Yet the kiss they'd shared, the heated moment they'd experienced the night in the bathroom when he'd found her bra, caused her cheeks to warm. "He's not the least bit interested in romance. Or in me."

Brian ran the knuckles of one hand along her cheek. "He has to be senile not to be."

A wad of uneasiness tumbled in her chest, but she shrugged it off and turned away from him, from a touch that might have set off a flurry of tingles a few days ago. Instead, it didn't sit well with her.

Outside, thunder boomed and rumbled, signaling the storm had hit. Inside, the phone on her desk rang.

She excused herself to answer it, glad to have an excuse to change the subject. "Daniela de la Cruz."

"Thank God," Clay said. "Dani, I need you. You've got to come home right now." The panic in his voice was almost palpable.

"What's the matter?"

"All hell broke loose, and I flipped out and sent Marcos and Delia to their rooms."

She glanced at Brian, saw him watching her intently. She knew she'd have to choose her words carefully. No one in the firm knew she was the guardian of three children who could drive a saint up the wall.

"That's a perfectly acceptable consequence, Mr. Callaghan."

"Oh, yeah? Well, I pretty much told them they could never come out."

She cleared her throat. "Yes, well, sometimes we all exaggerate. I'm sure that, when a suitable amount of time has passed—"

"Don't patronize me, Dani. I'm not sure who's in your office and making it hard for you to talk, but give them some excuse and come home now. I need you."

"What about the housekeeper?" she asked. "Can't she help?"

"Barbara went AWOL today."

"Well, what about Sara?" she asked.

"Anytime I walk anywhere near her, she looks at me as though I'm a time bomb ready to explode." Exasperation dripped off his voice.

"Are you?" she asked, wondering if he might really come unglued. Maybe it was his temper frightening him, as well as the children.

"Yeah. I'm ready to blow. And when I do, I'm going to come down there and tell Martin that he can kiss my ass goodbye. I'll find another firm, one who looks out for its clients. Come on, Dani. I've got you on retainer."

She blew out a sigh. "Okay. I'll be there in less than an hour."

When the line disconnected, she returned her gaze and her attention to Brian. "I'm sorry. Apparently, Mr. Callaghan is in a panic. He's threatening to find another law firm if I don't return. I've got the bulk of this brief finished, but you'll have to get one of the clerks to finish it for you."

Then she packed up her laptop and grabbed her purse.

"This is crazy," Brian said. "Why doesn't he hire a babysitter like other people do?"

Dani didn't respond. It wasn't that little baby causing all the trouble today. It was her siblings. The kids she was responsible for. The ones creating havoc with her life and her career.

She excused herself and went back to the ranch to face whatever it was that Clay couldn't—or *wouldn't*—handle. Forty-five minutes later she arrived, only to find the house quiet and Clay pacing the living room floor.

His gaze locked on hers. "I knew something like this would happen. I blew it."

She sat on the edge of the leather sofa in the family room. "What happened?"

"I was on the telephone, and the kids started arguing. I heard the baby cry out. Then Delia screamed, 'You're going to hurt her.' And the next thing I knew, this thing that looked just like Angela flew across the room. My heart went nuts, and I didn't realize it was that stupid baby doll..." He dragged a hand through his hair. "I don't lose control. I don't have a temper. I don't yell at small kids and dogs. But I just lost it."

"Where are Sara and the baby?" she asked.

"Right after I called you, Sara gave Angela a bottle, then put her to bed. I'm not sure where she is right now, but I suspect she's hiding in her room. And I can't blame her. She probably thinks I'm an ogre."

"And the other two?" she asked. "Are they still being punished?"

He nodded.

"When are they allowed out of their rooms?"

"Well, that's the problem. I was so frustrated that I told them they could spend the rest of their lives in there. Something tells me Dr. Spock or whoever is in charge of parenting rules these days would say that was a bit excessive. Wouldn't you agree?"

She appreciated his attempt at humor. "If it makes you feel better, I've had the same thing happen to me. It's a real ego blaster."

"I even cussed at them, which you probably don't approve of. But, hell, Dani, I'm not used to this."

"Don't be so hard on yourself." She reached out, grabbed his hand and gave it a squeeze.

He held on longer than necessary, as though needing some kind of parental infusion and appreciating her efforts to offer it to him. It was nice being part of a team for a change, even if it was only temporary. She wondered what it would be like having him—or anyone—in her corner on a daily basis.

"They probably hate me," he said. "On occasion, Trevor and I had a few run-ins, although not any as bad as this. I don't think he ever forgave me for them."

"Did he tell you why he didn't accept your apology?"

"No. I never actually said I was sorry."

"Weren't you?" she asked.

"Yeah. And he knew that."

"Did he?"

He studied her a moment, his hand still clutching hers. "Rex never used to apologize for anything because it was a sign of weakness. It made sense to me."

"Being *stubborn* is the real weakness," she said. "Are you sorry for losing your cool today?"

"Of course I am. The kids probably hate me now."

"Then I suggest you go upstairs and tell each one of them that you're sorry."

He released her hand, breaking the intimacy they shared. "If everything blows up in my face, I'll hold you accountable."

"And what if it works and makes everyone feel a lot better?"

He tossed her a wry grin. "Then I'll owe you one."

"You already do," she reminded him, wondering how they'd ever settle their debts.

Clay stood in Delia's room, where the six-year-old knelt near the bed holding her doll, and apologized for losing his temper.

"That's okay, Mr. Callaghan," little Delia said. "I forgive you for saying bad words and for getting mad at me when it was all Marcos' fault."

Then she wrapped her arms around his neck and gave him a hug that nearly squeezed the heart right out of him.

Next he knocked lightly on Sara's door, and she

told him to come in. He opened the door and found her sitting on top of the bed, her legs folded Indian-style and a teen fashion magazine on her lap.

She'd told him to enter, but he figured it would be easier for both of them if he remained in the doorway. "I, uh…I'm sorry for losing control. It isn't something I'm proud of. And I hope you won't hold it against me."

She grinned. "Hey, you saw me at my worst, too. Remember that first day we met? *You* didn't hold it against *me*."

He leaned against the doorjamb, pleased they'd found a common connection. "Yeah, well, thanks. And for what it's worth, after your sister takes you guys back home, you can come to the ranch and ride Bluebonnet anytime you want."

His words drew a bright-eyed smile that lit up the sparsely decorated guest room. Then she tossed the magazine aside, climbed from the bed and made her way toward him, reaching out to give him an appreciative hug.

He had half a notion to pull back as she approached, to put some distance between them, but he figured it would hurt her feelings. Besides, she seemed to believe he'd offered her the moon, rather than a tired-out old horse whose working days were over. So who was he to burst her bubble?

By the time he got to the room where Marcos waited, the bedroom that had once belonged to

Trevor, Clay was beginning to feel like an old hand at apologies. But somehow, being invited in and stepping over the threshold of this room brought back memories of words that shouldn't have been said, apologies that should have been made a long time ago.

Marcos, who sat on the floor near the closet that still held Trevor's things, gazed at him with red-rimmed eyes. "I'm really sorry, Mr. Callaghan. I didn't know you were on the telephone. And I didn't mean to tease my sister. But she…well, I…"

"You tease your sisters a lot," Clay said. "Why's that?"

Marcos shrugged. "I don't know. They're my sisters and all, but sometimes they really annoy me. It's not like I hate 'em. But you know how girls are, don't you?"

Clay wrestled with a smile, trying to remember how he felt about females when he was ten. He realized that, other than his mom, he hadn't had much use for them, either.

"Like Delia," Marcos explained. "She whines all the time and complains. And just 'cause she's little, everyone gives in to her. She used to be cool when she was a baby like Angela, but she's turning into a brat, and no one cares."

Clay thought about the girl who wore her long hair in pigtails most of the time. A six-year-old who'd just given him a hug that turned him inside out.

"Sara's only four years older than me," Marcos added. "But she thinks she's the boss of everything I say or do."

Clay could see where that would be troubling. He didn't like anyone telling him what to do, either.

Marcos sighed. "Don't the girls drive you crazy, too, Mr. Callaghan?"

At first Clay had expected them to. And today, when Marcos and Delia had fought, he'd nearly gone through the roof. But it wasn't *all* bad.

There were a couple of up sides, like the wonder he'd seen in Delia's eyes when she saw Mutt's puppies for the first time. Then there was the pure joy Sara had flashed the day she'd saddled Bluebonnet and mounted by herself. Clay had sensed her pride, as well as her love of horses.

"You know," Marcos said, "it would probably be better if Dani was home more. Having her gone so much is worse, now that my dad is dead…" The boy paused, then clamped his mouth shut and looked away. A moment later he wiped his forearm under his eyes.

Clay made his way to the bed. Then he sat on the edge of the mattress. "Women can be kind of annoying when they grow up, too. But mostly, it's because they're so different from us men."

"My dad said that, too. He said I'd grow up and appreciate them more someday. But I don't know. Maybe if they were like my mom used to be or the way Dani is, I wouldn't get so mad."

Clay thought about Dani, remembering the kiss they'd shared in Mexico, the bra she'd hung in his guest bathroom and the buzz of attraction that dogged him whenever she was near.

"Women are probably going to drive you crazy when you get older, too," Clay admitted. "But there's a whole lot to like about them."

"If my dad was around, it would be different. But you don't know how bad it is to live with a bunch of girls and be the only boy."

Nope. Clay didn't know how bad that was. If he were still ten, it would definitely be a pain in the butt.

"Maybe if you and I put our heads together, we can figure out a way to get along with the girls and not let them bother you."

"I don't know about that," the boy said.

"By the way," Clay said. "The reason I came in here was to apologize to you."

"Oh, yeah? Why?"

"Because I lost my temper and said things I didn't mean. I was frustrated about something else and snapped at you and Delia. It wasn't fair to either of you."

From his seat on the floor, Marcos pondered Clay's words, then looked up at him and grinned sagely. "I guess that's kind of like me getting mad at Delia or Sara when I'm really just mad about not having a dad or a brother or another boy to play with."

"Yeah," Clay said. "Just like that."

They sat there for a while, just the two of them. A boy and a man. Connecting in a way Clay had never connected with his son. Was it because he'd humbled himself and come to Marcos on a level that was different from any on which he'd ever approached Trevor? Or was it because Marcos wasn't the same kind of person Trevor had been? Maybe it was because Trevor's death had changed Clay a little.

He didn't know for sure, but he reached out a hand to Marcos and pulled him to a stand. "You know, it's kind of nice having another man around the house."

The boy brightened. "Yeah. I know just what you mean."

Clay hoped he did. Either way, he was glad he and Marcos had talked.

It hadn't done a damn thing to make him feel like he'd been a better father to Trevor. But at least he no longer felt like a complete parental failure.

Chapter Ten

A week after Angela arrived at the ranch, it was time for her to return to the doctor. Clay and Dani had taken her and had been delighted to learn that the baby was not only beginning to gain weight but was showing signs of improvement.

And what a relief that was.

To celebrate, Clay announced they would barbecue steaks and make homemade vanilla ice cream. The kids asked to invite Hawk, who'd become their buddy, and Clay agreed. Hawk had been happy to be included and drove out to the roadside market at Eden Corners, a small neighboring community, where he picked up ice and rock salt.

As Dani stood at the kitchen sink, rinsing leaves of romaine, a plump tomato, fresh mushrooms and a cucumber, Angela rocked slowly in the swing Dani had set up in the corner. Delia, who'd taken a special interest in the baby, chattered away, talking about one thing or another. Outside, the men stood over a custom-made, built-in barbecue and watched the steaks cook. And near the side of the house, the older children took turns cranking an old-fashioned ice cream maker that had to be forty or fifty years old. But according to Hawk, who'd found it in the barn, it still worked like a charm.

Earlier Clay had mixed up what he called his world-famous ice cream recipe, which called for a dozen eggs, sugar, half-and-half and vanilla, among other top-secret ingredients. Neither Dani nor the kids had ever eaten anything other than the store-bought variety, so they were looking forward to dessert this evening.

The potatoes were baking in the oven, so Dani's only other contribution was the salad. Since there'd been a collective effort to get the meal on the table, dinner seemed even more special.

Angela's improving health gave them much for which to be thankful. And so did the fact that she was eating better and had begun to show more interest in her surroundings and in the people who held her and answered her cries.

Yet there were other things—milestones, Dani

supposed—they also ought to celebrate. For one thing, Clay had always cared about the baby and had been clearly concerned about her, but up until now, his involvement had been from a distance. Lately she'd noticed him drawing closer, reaching out to Angela, even if it was only with the touch of a finger. Dani had also caught him whispering something to her once in a while, calling her Angie.

Okay, so he spoke to her in the same way he did to the dogs and puppies, but it was a start. And that, indeed, was something to celebrate.

After all, Dani needed to go back to work. And the faster grandfather and baby bonded, the sooner she could get her life back.

To make sure that happened, Dani had encouraged Clay to interview Linda Mahan, the woman who'd applied for the nanny position but couldn't start until she returned from her cruise. After going over the application, Dani had decided that Linda had the experience Clay needed, not to mention impeccable references.

Linda had Internet access aboard the ship, so Clay had e-mailed her and set up an appointment to meet upon her return. If everything went as expected, Dani and the kids would be going home in just over a week.

"She did it," Delia shrieked. "She really did it!"

Dani tore her gaze from the cutting board, where she chopped tomatoes for the salad. "What are you talking about, honey?"

"Angela *smiled* at me." Delia moved her mouth in a tight-lipped, dimpled grin, mocking what the baby had done. "Like this. See?"

The baby merely studied Delia now and showed no sign of a smile. But Dani set down the knife, washed her hands and wiped them on a dish towel. Then she strode toward the swing. Bending forward, she looked intently at Angela and grinned, as she'd done so many times in the past week.

"Hey, sweet girl," Dani said. "Did you smile at Delia?"

This time, the baby's lips twitched in a slight, upward tilt.

Okay, so it wasn't a full-blown smile, but it was a definite response—and a bigger one than any of them had ever drawn before.

"Well, I'll be darned," Dani said. "I think you're right, Delia."

"That's because God listened to me," the beaming child said. "I prayed that everyone would be happy again—like they used to be when Papa was alive. And I told him to make Angela be the happiest one of all."

Well, something was going on—miracle or not.

Delia, who'd been thrilled to have a real live baby to play with, had doted on Angela, even when the baby had given her less response than a doll. She deserved some credit, if not for her perseverance, then for her faith and prayer.

Angela had begun to connect with her caretakers.

"Should I tell Mr. Callaghan?" Delia asked.

"Sure, honey. Go ahead."

Dani watched as Delia dashed outside.

Delia tapped Clay on the arm and interrupted the conversation he was having with Hawk. But when he spotted her happy smile, he didn't have the heart to correct her.

"Guess what?" she asked.

Clay didn't have a clue. "You're going to have to give an old man a break and tell me."

"Angela smiled at me. She *really* did. And that means she knows that we love her." Even in the waning light of day, as dusk brought on the night, Clay could see excitement dance upon the child's face.

A surge of relief washed over him, even though he'd need to ask Dani about it. As badly as he wanted to believe Delia, he knew that children often saw things the way they wanted them to be.

Adults, too, he supposed.

"That's great," he told the little girl. "I'm glad to hear it."

"I'm going to tell Marcos and Sara." Then she dashed to the side of the patio, where her big sister and brother were turning the crank on the old ice cream maker.

"You know," Hawk said, "it's been kind of nice having those little rugrats underfoot."

There'd been a few good moments, Clay supposed, as well as a couple of trying ones. But all in all, the kids seemed to be enjoying their time at the ranch—thank goodness for that. He suspected any one of them could have made life hell if they'd been unhappy here.

"Sara has flat-out blossomed," Hawk said.

Clay agreed. "She'd been giving Dani a lot of trouble at home, but she's been a real help around here. To tell you the truth, I'm pleasantly surprised."

"Yeah, and she's got a gift with horses, too. You might think about taking her to see Wanda Patterson."

"The barrel racer?" Clay asked.

"Well, I'm not suggesting Sara would be interested in learning how to ride in the rodeo, or that she'd ever be able to reach a level where she could actually compete. But she might enjoy meeting Wanda and seeing all the ribbons and trophies in her case."

"Have you seen Wanda's awards?" Clay asked.

Hawk shrugged. "A time or two."

Wanda had lost her husband, and Clay knew she and Hawk had gone to the same support group down at the community church. He wondered if the two...

Aw, heck. That was Hawk's business.

"Wanda's a good woman," Hawk added. "It might be nice for her to have visitors. She's been holed up in her house grieving for too dang long."

Clay shrugged. "I guess it wouldn't hurt to introduce her to Sara. But Dani and the kids won't be around much longer."

"Well, at least Sara's been here long enough for ol' Bluebonnet to work her magic."

"That's for sure." Clay poked the center steak with the barbecue fork and flipped it over. "She's had a big change in her attitude, and I'd hate to see her backslide once she goes home."

"Maybe you ought to just give her Bluebonnet," Hawk said.

"I would. But Dani and the kids live in the city and don't have a place to keep a horse." Clay thought on it for a moment. "I suppose she could keep it here. Poor old Bluebonnet would probably appreciate that. She hasn't gotten this much attention since Rex died."

Hawk chuckled. "You know, boss, Bluebonnet's not the only thing that's been responsible for an attitude adjustment. Those kids have worked on yours, too."

"What do you mean?"

"You've loosened up. The last time I had my sister's kids out here, you were on edge the whole time. That's how things started out this past week, but look at you now."

"Look at what?"

"Well, for one thing, Marcos shadowed you all day today, whether you were driving to the feedlot or riding fences. It didn't seem to bother you none. In fact, I think you kind of liked it."

Clay shrugged. "It didn't bother me. And you've got a point. I seem to be relating a heck of a lot better to these kids than I ever did to my own son."

"Maybe it's because you're not trying to make them into something they're not."

Like Clay had done with Trevor.

Hawk adjusted the hat on his head. "There's an old saying from the Bible that says you should train up a child in the way he should go."

Clay wasn't a religious man. Not like Hawk, whose faith had actually grown stronger after losing his wife and the full use of his leg. And he wasn't sure where Hawk was going with all this.

"I'm afraid I don't get your point," Clay admitted. "I take it a parent ought to set an example and teach a kid right from wrong."

"Yep, that, too. But it also means a parent ought to raise a kid in the way the kid is meant to go, not in the way a parent wants him to go. The trick is to study the child and figure out what his God-given talent is and where his dream is going to lead him."

Clay had pretty much come to that conclusion— eventually. He and his son had butted heads when he'd tried to make a rancher out of him. But once he'd given up and let the boy choose the college he wanted to attend, as well as the major he wanted to pursue, things had gotten...better, he supposed.

Had Clay been wrong to push the ranch on him, even though it had been Trevor's legacy?

That didn't quite compute to Clay, especially when the boy would have inherited the ranch someday. Yet he suspected Hawk had a point.

Too bad there wasn't a damn thing he could do about it now.

The usual guilt that plagued him kicked up a notch and stole the joy he'd been feeling.

Later that evening, after they'd all pitched in and done the dishes and the kids had gone to bed, Dani took a shower. Then she put on her nightgown, slipped into her robe and, as had become her custom when the house had quieted down for the evening, walked out onto the front porch and relished the sounds of the ranch at night.

A horse whinnied in the distance, and crickets chirped near the barn. The scent of a night-blooming jasmine she'd spotted the second evening here, filled the cool night air.

As much as she wanted to get back to the office, back to the environment where she felt most competent, there was a freedom at the ranch she didn't have anywhere else. A freedom from the need to hold everything together.

Maybe it was because the kids were happy here—or at least, happy to be on a vacation. Or maybe it was having another adult around. Someone to balance out the power struggles that seemed to batter her when she least needed the extra stress.

In a sense, her life seemed to be oddly on track now. Even Clay, whose quiet, peaceful ranch had been overrun with kids this past week, appeared to be adjusting to the ragtag little family that had practically moved in.

Of course, this was all temporary.

The door squeaked open, and she turned to see Clay.

"Do you mind if I join you out here?" he asked. "Or would you rather be alone?"

She'd come outside for some quiet time, but he wasn't intruding. Not at all. "Come on out."

"Delia said the baby smiled at her," he said.

"I missed it. But I could have sworn I got a similar response from her this evening, too. I think it's working, Clay. She's feeling loved, and she's connecting."

"That's good news." He stepped up beside her, his arm brushing against hers, and leaned against the railing, as she was doing.

She caught a whiff of his musky scent, and a rush of arousal swirled around her, making her aware of the fact that under her robe she wore a thin cotton gown. And under that, she was naked.

As wrong as Clay was for her, as impossible as a relationship might be, that didn't mean she wasn't attracted to him. That she didn't wish he'd kiss her again.

She looked up at the sky, where a sliver of a moon

shone in the midst of a scatter of glittering stars, setting off something magical in the heavens. And something warm and enchanting in her.

"It's a pretty night," she said.

"Yeah."

They stood like that for a while, silent and full of thought.

"Marcos asked me to show him how to rope a calf this morning," Clay said. "So we worked on it a little."

"Thanks. I appreciate the time you've been spending with him."

"It's a fair trade. I appreciate the time you're spending with the baby." He cast her a shadowed smile.

"But I'm getting paid for my work."

"Don't worry about it."

She wasn't. Not really.

He returned his focus to the heavens, but his words remained on the here and now. "I'd like to give Bluebonnet to Sara, but thought I should ask you first."

She shot him a glance. "Are you serious? We don't have anyplace to keep a horse. And then there's the expense…"

Clay turned to face her, yet still leaned against the porch railing. "She can keep the horse here. I don't care. Besides, Bluebonnet used to belong to Rex. I'd rather not put her out to pasture and forget all about her. I'm not sure if you've noticed or not, but Sara is crazy about Bluebonnet and an old horse can't ask for more than that."

"Yes, I've noticed." Dani fingered the knot that held the sash of her robe. "In fact, she'd been working on my father to let her get a horse right before he died."

"If you agree, you might notice a change in her."

"I already have noticed a big one. And I thank you for that."

"It was a fluke. I had no idea she'd respond favorably."

They talked for a while, sharing the kinds of things two parents might at the end of the day.

While lying in bed, she supposed.

The thought of removing her robe and joining Clay in the middle of a king-size bed, feeling his warmth, cuddling and drawing strength from each other, crept over her. Her gaze sought his, finding him studying her in a similar manner. At least, it felt that way.

Theirs was a weird relationship. Client and attorney. Man and woman. Temporary parents who'd joined forces for the good of the brood.

But she realized it was more than the kids that had made her grow easy with him, more than the kiss they'd shared stirring her hormones and triggering her desire to kiss him again. She actually could imagine herself falling for him if things were different.

He turned to her, cupped her jaw and brushed a calloused thumb across her skin. Her heart skipped a beat, and arousal built in a steady rush, battering the walls she'd fought hard to build.

She shouldn't get involved with him—or with any man, for that matter—until she no longer had the responsibility of the kids. Yet the urge to do so anyway crept over her when she considered the shared parenting they'd been involved in, the crazy roles they'd been playing; when she thought about his rough and tough exterior and saw signs of tenderness underneath.

"I swore I wouldn't get this close to you again," he said, gaze locked on hers, hearts thumping in time. "That I wouldn't touch you and think about kissing you again."

"And I swore I wouldn't let you."

Neither of them moved or even dared to breathe, yet desire flared between them.

When Clay had first stepped outside to catch some fresh air and realized Dani was on the porch, he'd been torn between honoring her privacy and giving in to some dumb urge to stay and talk with her, to hear her voice, catch the lemon blossom scent of her shampoo. In spite of his better judgment, he'd joined her.

Now look at him.

Damn. He should have run for the hills while he had a chance.

He knew he'd have regrets in the morning, but

right now all he wanted to do was drink her in and savor her taste. And the fact that she wasn't fighting him off, wasn't even pulling back, didn't help.

They remained rooted to the floor, gazes locked, his fingers splayed against her neck, the silky strands of her hair brushing his knuckles.

Still, neither of them moved.

Not until her mouth parted, and she brushed the tip of her tongue across her lips.

That was all it took. Clay was lost. He pulled her to him, her mouth to his, taking what he'd claimed in Mexico.

The kiss deepened into something wild and reckless, as he tasted every moist, velvety nook and cranny in her mouth. Yet, try as he might, he couldn't get enough.

His hands slid along the curve of her back, the slope of her hips, and a rush of desire nearly knocked him senseless. He gripped her derriere and pulled her against him.

She moaned into his mouth, driving him wild with need.

He'd merely hoped to have a repeat of the last kiss, but this one was more powerful, more blood stirring, which scared the bejeezus out of him.

He wasn't sure what frightened him more, the lust she stirred in him, or the emotion she evoked. Lord knew he wasn't the kind of guy who could give a woman what she needed, other than in bed. And worse, he wasn't the kind of guy who could settle down, especially with a woman who had three kids to raise.

So in spite of a demanding arousal, and a frustrated libido that wasn't going to give him a minute's rest, he broke the kiss.

Yet he still held her close.

Their breaths, hot and ragged, reminded him of everything he'd ever given up, everything he'd ever lost. Yet he didn't possess the courage to push for more than he deserved.

"I'm sorry," he said. "I wanted to do that so bad that I couldn't see straight. I didn't think about the repercussions."

She didn't comment, and he wasn't sure if that was a good thing or not.

Clay didn't get emotionally involved with anyone, never had, never would. As much as he wanted to take her inside, to take her to his bed, he couldn't risk hurting her.

"I'm not the kind of man you need," he admitted, "I don't make romantic commitments."

She stepped back, crossed her arms and lifted her chin. The desire and passion that had brewed in her eyes moments ago had been replaced with a different flame, a spark of anger.

"I don't think you have any idea what I'm looking for in a man, Clay. Especially since I don't even know that myself. I have a law degree I fought long and hard to get and a promising career. I'm also responsible for three children, so I'd be pretty stupid to get mixed up with anyone right now."

Clay nodded, as though he understood. As though he didn't realize it wasn't anger speaking out; it was pain. He'd hurt her feelings, which was the last thing in the world he'd wanted to do.

Yet he was too afraid to broach the obvious—even though the truth was floundering around in his own mind.

There was more than lust drawing him to her.

But he'd be damned if he'd do anything about it.

Chapter Eleven

The urge to let Clay have it—verbally or otherwise—had taunted Dani all through the night and into the next morning.

After that earthshaking, knee-buckling kiss that rivaled any Dani had ever had or hoped to have, Clay had ended things abruptly.

I'm not the kind of man you need.

I don't make romantic commitments.

What had he meant by that?

She hadn't asked for anything; he hadn't even given her the chance. Sure, the thought had crossed her mind and was appealing, but she'd never seriously considered it.

So when he'd pulled away, he'd left her a lot to deal with in very short order.

The kiss for one thing. And a blinding surge of desire that had tempted her to throw caution to the wind.

Then being backed into a corner.

Up until a few days ago, she'd been determined to focus on the kids, rather than a male/female relationship—and she still was. There was only so much time in a day, and between her family at home and her work at the office, Dani could barely spare five minutes for a long, hot soak in the tub, let alone for a date.

But when Clay ended the kiss—as well as any misplaced notions—he hadn't given her time to rally her spinning senses. He'd just made the call for both of them.

Shoot, she wasn't up for a love affair, either.

But what in the world were they going to do with that darned attraction to each other? Tiptoe around it until Mrs. Mahan got home from her cruise?

By the time Dani had returned to her room last night, she was fuming—both at Clay and at herself. She'd run through script after script of should-have-saids and wished-she'd-saids. As a result, she hadn't fallen asleep until well after midnight.

She'd told Clay that she didn't want a relationship, which had been true. But after that blood-rushing, conscience-battering kiss, which had been far more arousing than their first, her hormones had been ready to revolt.

To be honest, she would have let the kiss go on much longer than it had. Not that she'd meant to drag him off to bed. She wouldn't have let it go that far, but Clay had ended it before she'd been able to do so herself.

And she would have. Really.

After all, Clay was a client, for goodness sake, and not the kind of man she'd planned to ever get involved with romantically.

Still, she suspected there was more going on between her and Clay than plain old biology, and when push came to shove, she believed he was struggling with it all, too.

Last night he'd admitted to the growing attraction, as well as the results of giving in to physical urges. Okay, so he also had more willpower than she had.

Or maybe his fear of getting involved with a woman responsible for so many kids had been more effective than a cold shower.

Great. That was a real ego booster, even though she'd been avoiding relationships for the same reason.

This morning, when she'd come downstairs to get a bottle for Angela, Clay had already made coffee and left, so she'd fixed herself a cup before scrambling eggs for the kids. All the while, she was both glad that he wasn't around and annoyed because he was avoiding her.

So when the telephone rang at just before noon, and she recognized Brian Westlake's voice, her own tone took on far more enthusiasm than she felt. "Hey, Brian. How are things going?"

"Great. The Gridleys' attorney approached me about a settlement."

That was exciting news. The case they'd been working on was as good as done. The only thing that would have made it better was to have been in the office when that particular call had come in.

"Thanks for letting me know," she said.

"You're welcome. But there's something else I wanted to run by you."

Assuming it was work related, she said, "Sure. Go ahead."

"How about dinner and the theater next Saturday night?" he asked. "To celebrate how well we work together."

Indecision swirled over her, and silence clogged the line. She had a soaring urge to prove to Brian there wasn't anything going on with Clay, not to mention wanting to show Clay the same thing.

And, she realized, maybe she needed to convince herself as well.

"A night out sounds wonderful, Brian. The new nanny won't start for a while, so I'll have to find someone else to come in and help. But leave that to me. I'll orchestrate something."

They were all getting used to the baby's schedule,

so maybe Sara would be able to handle things while Dani was gone. After all, the baby went to bed early and slept through the night.

"Good," Brian said. "I'll pick you up at seven."

Uh-oh. Not at her house. She didn't want word to get out at the office about where she lived and with whom. So she came up with another plan. "I'll be at the ranch. So why don't I meet you in town?"

"All right. How about La Belle's?"

It was one of the nicest restaurants in Houston, and the fact that Brian was trying to go all out ought to please her, even if dinner and the theater weren't nearly as appealing as they should be.

"Perfect. I'll see you there." Then she hung up the telephone, more conflicted than ever. Because, deep inside, she wished it had been Clay asking her out on Saturday night. Clay who was making his interest known.

And that bothered her more than she cared to admit.

Talk about a relationship being star-crossed.

Before she could stew about her feelings for Clay any longer, the back door swung open and footsteps sounded on the service porch.

"Hey," Clay said.

Startled and jumpy, she jerked back, assuming he was talking to her, until he finished the sentence.

"How're those babies doing, Mutt?"

Dani clamped her mouth shut, which meant his question was met with silence.

When he entered the kitchen and their gazes met, the stillness was almost overwhelming.

He cleared his throat. "Hawk just left for Galveston. His sister is in the hospital having an emergency appendectomy, and he had to go pick up her kids. He'll be bringing them back here for a few days."

More kids?

Clay, who kept his emotions reined in, ought to be climbing the walls before the weekend. "How many are there?"

"Two. Toby is about Sara's age, and Kendra is a couple of years younger."

"How long will they be here?"

"At least until Sunday. But I figure, between you, Hawk and me, we ought to be able to keep them from hurting each other. Or us."

Clay might be paying top dollar for her "services," but even an attorney deserved a night off. "Well, you men are on your own Saturday afternoon and evening. I've got a date."

The look on his face—the parted lips, the hint of stupor—was priceless, whether she could accurately read his mind or not.

She wasn't sure if it was fear of having Angela on his own or a pang of jealous surprise that Dani had a date, but she didn't stick around long enough to figure it out.

Instead she turned and walked away, wishing she could see his expression.

And glad he couldn't see hers.

* * *

Kendra and Toby, Hawk's niece and nephew, were nice kids. There may have been a couple of shy, awkward moments upon their arrival, but they soon hit it off with Marcos and Sara.

"You know," Hawk told Clay, as the children stood near the corral and studied the horses in the waning afternoon sunlight, "I was thinking. Maybe I ought to take these rascals camping down by the lake. It'll be fun for them, plus it'll keep them out of your hair for a day or so."

Before Clay could respond, Sara chimed in. "Can Bluebonnet come, too?"

Clay had yet to give the okay, but to be honest, he thought Hawk's idea a good one.

As a boy, he used to spend his free time—what little he'd had—out at the fishing hole. And as far as Bluebonnet went, she'd be a good sport no matter where Sara took her. "Sure, Hawk. And taking the horse is up to you."

In less than an hour, the boys helped Hawk pack their gear and pile it in the back of the pickup, while the girls and Dani gathered food for them to take along.

Even little Delia, who'd been torn between joining in with the bigger kids and sticking close to home, decided to leave both her doll and Angela in Dani's care, then climbed into the cab of the truck.

Hawk loaded Bluebonnet into a trailer so Sara

could ride once they arrived, then slid behind the wheel of the pickup. Before starting the engine, he looked at Dani and grinned. "I'm not sure why you packed all that food. We'll be feasting on grilled trout tonight."

As Clay watched them drive away, he realized the house would be quiet again this evening. But that also meant he and Dani would be tripping over each other and fighting the attraction that was about to drive him mad.

"Do you think he can handle all those kids?" Dani asked.

"Yep. Hawk's a big kid himself. He'll do a lot better with them than either of us would do."

"You're probably right." She placed her hands on her hips then stretched the kinks from her back, a movement that drew his attention to her full breasts, small waist and denim-clad hips. A sensual movement that was far more intriguing than it ought to be.

"What do you want for dinner?" she asked.

"It doesn't matter."

"I have a couple of leftover steaks I can warm up. And I can make a potato-cheese casserole. Maybe some green beans?"

It sounded good. Even more delicious than last night's meal. Besides, Clay was hungry. He'd skipped breakfast in an effort to avoid facing Dani.

Now look at them. They were together.

And alone.

Of course, she didn't seem to be too caught up in the kiss they'd shared, the one he'd put a halt to before he'd gotten carried away, scooped her into his arms and carried her off to bed.

Ending things had seemed like a hell of a good idea last night. But as he'd headed back to his room and the empty, king-size bed, he'd had second thoughts. He'd been left with a niggling sense of regret that had dogged him into the next day.

Hell, Dani was a woman of the new millennium. A career woman by her own assessment. She also had a date on Saturday night, which meant she hadn't put too much stock in that kiss. So why the panic on his part? Why had he hedged the emotional stuff?

Maybe she'd be interested in having a no-strings-attached sexual fling that would sate their needs.

Of course, he'd have to figure out a way to ask her.

Too bad he'd backed off last night. It would have been the perfect opportunity to bring up the subject. Hopefully, it hadn't been his one and only chance.

If so, he was afraid he might have blown it.

After putting Angela to bed in her crib, Dani puttered around in the kitchen, creating a brand-new meal out of leftovers.

She and Clay had avoided each other all afternoon, and just recently he'd headed upstairs for a shower. Being here alone with him seemed odd. Just the two of them, a man and a woman.

She imagined that eating indoors, with walls that could close in on them, would make things more awkward. So she stepped out on the back porch, deciding to set the glass-top patio table. The window overhead was open, allowing Dani to hear Angela, in case she cried out.

Even though the porch light provided a soft glow, Dani decided to add candles and brought out several that had lined the fireplace mantel. She placed them in the center of the table, then lit them with matches she'd found in the kitchen drawer.

As she admired the warm ambiance, footsteps alerted her to Clay's approach, and she caught a taunting whiff of his masculine scent—musk and soap. She turned and found him standing in the open sliding door, a bottle of red wine in one hand and two glasses in the other.

"I wondered where you'd slipped off to," he said. "I wanted to ask if you'd like to have a drink before dinner."

Was this the same man who'd withdrawn from her last night?

She didn't answer right away. For some reason she couldn't. As he leaned in the doorway, fresh from the shower, his hair still damp, she couldn't help staring, admiring him and noting that he hadn't shaved. The light stubble gave him a rugged, reckless appearance. Edgy and dangerous.

She tucked a strand of hair behind her ear and nodded toward the candles flickering on the table. "I probably ought to pass on the wine. After what happened last time…"

Guadalajara came to mind, reminding her of their first kiss and mingling with the memory of the kiss they'd shared less than twenty-four hours ago.

He tossed her a crooked grin. "I won't let you have too much tonight."

"The only reason I let you talk me into a drink before was because of the turbulence and the weather."

Yet there seemed to be another storm brewing, another reason to dull her senses.

He pulled out a chair for her, and when she sat, he poured two glasses, filling hers halfway. Then he took a seat across from her, leaned back in his seat and stretched out his legs.

"How'd you sleep last night?" he asked.

"Excuse me?"

"After that kiss. Did it keep you awake, too?"

She didn't want to admit that it had, nor did she understand why he'd broached the subject that had made them both uneasy, so she kept quiet.

"I need to tell you something, Dani. I've been having second thoughts."

"About what?"

"About ignoring the heat that's brewing between us."

Where was he going with this conversation?

"You can't deny what's happening," he said.

"You mean the attraction we're feeling? No, I can't do that."

"I know that if we decide to get involved sexually, it could complicate things for us, at least until Mrs. Mahan gets here and I, hopefully, decide to hire her."

That was a given.

"But I wish we would have let that kiss play out last night. And for what it's worth, I wouldn't be opposed to taking things to a sexual level."

The idea was tossed out on the table like a business offer, but she supposed that was better than playing games, hemming and hawing.

So was she up for a sexual relationship?

A warm buzz in her veins was enough to stimulate a few fantasies of her own. It had been so long since she'd been with a man in that way. And she hadn't expected to have the chance for quite a while.

Clay reached across the table, taking her hand in his. "It would be good between us."

If the staggering heat of their kisses was any indication, he was right on the money.

He gave her hand a warm, gentle squeeze that sent a whisper of heat along her arms until it wrapped around her heart and kicked up her pulse. "So, what do you say?"

"Can I think about it?"

"Sure." A smile lit his eyes. "We've got all night."

They both chose that moment to take a sip of wine. And when their eyes met, her arousal surged, as did the anticipation in the air.

She'd told him she would think about it. And that's exactly what she was doing. But she wasn't contemplating a decision about whether or not she wanted to make love with him. *That* choice had been determined the moment Clay had made the suggestion.

But could she handle a no-strings-attached, one-shot deal?

What happened if she developed feelings for a man who, by his own admission, didn't get emotionally involved with his lovers?

It seemed, at this moment, that she could. And she had to face the fact that her no-dating-clients rule was an excuse not to risk getting involved with a man who couldn't handle the kids or, more important, a man who couldn't make an emotional commitment to her.

But right now her options were limited.

She could either make love with Clay or remain celibate until Delia donned a high school cap and gown, which was only a mere twelve years from now.

Perish the thought.

Of course, there was also that dinner and theater date with Brian waiting in the wings. But for some reason, that evening, with all its promised glitz and glamour, paled next to this one.

Was that because this was so immediate?

Or because Clay's kiss was so arousing?

Either way, she was going to need a little romance, some foreplay.

And a lot more of his knee-weakening kisses.

"Excuse me for a minute." He got to his feet, then strode inside the house. Before long, the sound of a country love song drifted out to the patio. When he returned, he stood beside the table and held out a hand to her. "Dance with me."

Who was this man? And what had he done with her client, the brooding rancher who made sex sound like a business arrangement?

"Are you kidding?" she asked.

"You don't like dancing?"

"No. Yes. I mean…" She took his hand and let him pull her up. And into his arms.

They fit together perfectly. As they swayed to the seductive beat, one of his hands held hers against his chest, while the other warmed the small of her back and pressed her close.

Hormones and pheromones sparked the air around them like a swarm of fireflies.

She rested her head against his cheek, feeling the

warmth of his breath upon her neck. She inhaled slowly and deeply, relishing the musky, soap-laced scent that belonged only to him.

When the last chords of the song drifted away, he cupped her cheeks with his hands. His gaze, clouded with desire, snaked around her, holding her tight. All she wanted was his arms around her again, to feel his lips on hers. So she reached up and drew his mouth to hers.

The kiss instantly deepened, and as their tongues began to mate, he pulled her against him. She felt the hardness of his erection and sensed the depth of his need.

As they continued to taste, to seek, to savor, she whimpered, revealing that she was as aroused as he. That she was ready to take a sexual leap. But this time she was the first to pull away, to stop the sweet assault on her senses.

"Okay," she said, her voice ragged and wispy.

"Is something wrong?"

Desire and longing glazed his eyes, and she knew he saw the same in hers.

"I think it's time that we went into the house. And into the bedroom."

A hot and heavy rush, the likes of which Clay hadn't experienced in a long time—*if ever*—surged through him, and he reached for her hand and grinned. "Honey, at this moment, I'd follow you any-where."

They held hands as they walked up the stairs to his bedroom and made their way along the hallway. Although her steps didn't falter, she tugged at his arm as if having second thoughts.

When he stole a glance at her, she flushed a deep shade of pink. "It's been a long time since I've made love with anyone."

Her words took him aback, making him wonder whether she'd had much experience. For some reason, her virginal shyness made her and what they were about to do all the more special.

He longed to have her, but he wouldn't push. He'd take things slow and easy, savoring each moment and making sure it was not only good for her, but much better than she remembered.

"It's been a while for me, too," he admitted, as he led her into the master bedroom with its four-poster bed, bold red comforter and dark oak furniture. "But I have a feeling it will all come back to us."

Once inside, he turned to face her and took her hands in his. The longing in her eyes nearly knocked him to the floor. He'd planned to take his time, but as her lips parted, his control faded into the passion-charged air, and he pulled her into his arms, claiming her as his own.

The kiss deepened, and their hands roamed, explored, stroked.

She leaned into him, pressing and rubbing herself

against his erection until his testosterone level peaked and nearly took his breath away.

He longed to bury himself deep within her, and he wasn't sure how much longer he could wait.

She whimpered, threading her fingers in his hair and gripping him with desperation.

As their mouths locked in a kiss, a moan formed low in his throat. He wanted to feel more of her— skin to skin, breasts to chest. He fumbled with the buttons of the spring-green blouse she wore, hoping he didn't rip it in the process.

It might be wise to remove his mouth from her lips long enough to undress, but for the life of him, he couldn't stop until he got his fill of the intoxicating kiss. Or his fill of *her.*

So much for taking it slow and easy.

She drew away long enough to whisper, "I'll take it off."

He stared at her, caught in an arousal of epic proportions, enamored by the provocative way she stripped off her blouse and let it flutter to the floor. Next she unzipped her jeans, then slid them over her hips and peeled them off.

When she stood before him in a pair of lacy white panties and a matching bra, virginal in color, he swallowed hard, and his heart pounded out a primal, sexual beat that urged him to remove his shirt.

He eased toward her, slowly. Almost reverently. "You're beautiful, Dani."

"So are you."

He could almost believe she meant it, and a grin—probably goofy—spread across his face.

She skimmed her fingers across his chest, sending a shiver through his nerve endings and a shimmy of heat through his blood. Then she reached behind her and unhooked her bra, making it clear that she wanted him as badly as he wanted her.

Next she slid the straps over her shoulders, letting the fancy piece of satin and lace drop to the floor, revealing her breasts. He ached to touch them, to caress them. To lay claim to her body, at least for tonight. So he bent and took a nipple in his mouth, tasting, suckling, taunting.

Dani gasped in pleasure, as Clay worked his magic, and her knees nearly buckled. He was not only a good lover, he was considerate, too, giving her a glimpse into the inner man.

A woman would be lucky to claim him as her own.

He scooped her into his arms and carried her to the bed, where he slipped off her panties and continued to stroke, caress and kiss her senseless. He loved her with his mouth and his hands, taking his time to pleasure her.

While he drove her wild with an aching sexual need, she forgot all about the future she had carefully planned and the kind of man with whom she would fall in love someday. Instead, she entertained images of herself and Clay.

It was crazy.

But she couldn't imagine making love to anyone else ever again.

Was it possible that she was falling for him? A man who fought emotional commitment?

If she told herself no, she'd be lying. She'd seen him mellow with the kids, seen him lower his guard and reveal the man inside.

Could his feelings for Dani change his attitude about love and commitment? If so, something romantic could develop between them. Something lasting.

After tonight their lives would never be the same again. And quite frankly, Dani wasn't sure if she cared.

She'd never been so bold when it came to love-making before, but she'd never ached so badly for a man, either.

Yet it was more than Clay's caress that she needed, more than his kiss.

How much more—in a romantic sense—was left to be seen, but she'd settle for what she could have right now. And that was having him inside her, sliding in and out, filling her to the brim, relieving the emptiness she feared she would have for years to come.

She wanted to touch him, too. To taste and stroke. To drive him wild with desire.

She grappled with his zipper, and as her fingers brushed against his erection, he shuddered. Then he dug through the drawer in the nightstand and pulled out a condom.

In no more than the blink of an eye and the beat of a heart, they were both naked.

He tore open the foil packet.

"Let me help." She took the protection from him, surprising herself, and reached for him, stroking his length.

She glanced up at his face, saw his eyes closed in pleasure as she rolled on the condom, her hands and fingers lingering, caressing.

She was going to remember this night forever, but she didn't dare say a word, didn't dare wish or hope for anything more than this sweet joining.

Clay rolled her to her back and hovered over her. As she opened for him, she braced her hands upon his hips, and he entered her. She arched up to meet him, taking all he had to offer, giving everything she had.

He thrust deeply, in and out. Her body responded to his, melding, molding, until she reached a mountainous peak and cried out with a mind-spinning climax. He shuddered, releasing along with her, as they held on tight, rising and falling with each wave of pleasure.

She didn't know what tomorrow would bring.

But tonight she'd touched the moon and stars.

And no one else had ever taken her anywhere close.

Chapter Twelve

As the dawn crept through a crack in the curtains, Clay and Dani lay cuddled in his bed. He drew her close to his chest and savored the fragrance of her shampoo, the faint whiff of her perfume.

Last night had been one of those once-in-a-lifetime experiences. A blood-stirring memory that would make him smile, long after she went back home.

And that's what had him stymied. Unbalanced. Wanting to tighten his armor a notch.

Somewhere between midnight and dawn, she'd touched something inside of him, something no one else ever had. Something that ought to scare the spit right out of him, if he'd let it.

Her bottom nestled in his lap, and he felt himself stirring, rising to the occasion...again. But since they'd gone through every last condom he'd had during the night, he'd better get his lust under control.

She looked especially pretty this morning, with her hair splayed on his pillow, the rumpled sheets lying around them. The scent of their lovemaking lingered in the air, and in spite of the emotional shield he always piled on after a climax, he hadn't actually withdrawn from her last night. It was only now that he was wondering why, which should be kicking up a flurry of butterflies in his gut.

Clay didn't make commitments. He didn't let sex influence his better judgment.

In fact, after spending the night with a lover, they never faced the dawn together. He was usually long gone by then, which made it easier to keep relationships superficial. But there was no place he wanted to run off to today—other than a drugstore so that he could purchase more condoms.

So this was a first.

From down the hall, he heard the baby fuss. His initial thought had been to nudge Dani awake, to let her know that Angela needed to eat. But he just couldn't bring himself to disturb her. Not yet. Not while she wore a sweet, sated expression, even in sleep.

He slowly slid his arm from under her head, trying

not to wake her, then he carefully rolled out of bed, slipped on his jeans and headed for Angela's room.

When he stood over the crib, the baby studied him. He didn't see any sign of the smile she'd blessed Delia with, but she made eye contact—something she hadn't done at first.

"Hey, Angie. Why don't we let Dani sleep for a while. If you promise not to tell—or complain—I'll take you into the kitchen and feed you. But no diaper changing, okay?" He picked up the baby, thinking she was pretty floppy and hoping he wasn't squeezing her too hard. The doctor had said she was gaining weight, but, damn, she was small.

He carried her into the kitchen, and he appreciated her not screaming. If she knew how little experience he had with babies, she'd be squawking to beat the band.

Okay. Now what?

He wasn't sure if he could juggle her while fixing the bottle, so he placed her in the swing. "Be a good sport, Angie. I'm just going to warm up the stuff, okay?"

She didn't respond, but followed his movements, which he figured was a good thing. Moments later, he had the bottle ready.

Clay was tempted to take her out of the swing, but figured she was safer there. So he stood in front of her and held the bottle, watching her chow down.

When she finished, he withdrew the nipple from

her mouth and could have sworn he saw the flicker of a grin. For a moment he wanted to tell Dani. But he hated to get goofy over something he might have imagined. So he pulled her from the swaying cloth seat and carried her back to the crib.

"Is something wrong?" Dani asked from his bed down the hall, her voice sleepy soft.

"Nope."

"Is the baby okay?"

"Yeah. Quiet as a little mouse." And stuffed to the gills.

He was actually proud of himself, but knew better than to brag about his efforts to mimic what he'd seen Dani do.

After laying Angela on her back in the crib, he studied the colorful mobile that was attached to the rail. There was a switch on the side. When he flipped it on, a circus tune began to play, while five dangling bears in bright-pink tutus circled.

"What are you doing?" Dani asked, still down the hall.

He returned to the master bedroom and spotted her sitting in bed, the sheets pulled to her breasts, covering what he'd already seen, what he'd claimed as his own. He shot her a grin. "Buying us some more time to lounge in bed, I suppose."

Dani's heart swelled to overflowing as she studied the bare-chested, denim clad cowboy standing in the doorway. "You fed the baby?"

"Yeah, but don't tell anyone." He sauntered toward her, the top button of his jeans undone and looking as sexy as a man ever had. "And don't expect that to happen all the time."

"I won't say a word, but I do expect you to start doing more and more."

"Well, I had selfish motives," he said with a wink. "I wanted more time with you."

Had he found another condom? She didn't think so, which was too bad. She made room for him on the bed, and he stretched out on top of the sheets and propped himself up on an elbow.

The fact that he wanted to be with her was touching. And sweet. It was also evidence that he was feeling the same way about her as she was about him.

Something wonderful had happened last night, and she wasn't just talking about great sex. If there'd ever been a question in her heart before, there wasn't any longer. Dani had fallen in love with the stubborn rancher, a man who was evolving into a dream come true. She wanted to fall asleep in his arms every night, to wake to his grin each day.

After a long, lingering kiss that made her wish he'd found a case of condoms, she climbed from bed. She wanted a shower but needed to check Angela first. So she picked up the chambray shirt Clay had discarded on the floor last night and slipped it on. Then she went to the room she shared with the baby. "Good morning, sunshine."

Dani was met with the sweetest smile she'd ever seen. It was more than a quirk of the lips this time. The loving response shot straight through Dani's heart.

"Clay?" she called. "Come here, will you?"

Moments later he joined her by the crib, his face sober, his brow furrowed. "What's the matter? Did I do something wrong?"

"No, not at all. Just watch this." Dani proceeded to baby talk and coax another smile from Angela.

A heartbeat later, they were both rewarded with glimmering little eyes and a toothless grin.

"She's going to be all right," Dani said, turning to Clay and wrapping her arms around him. "Thank God."

"And thank *you*," he said. "I don't know what I would have done without you."

"So where do we go from here?" Dani asked, meaning more than caring for Angela. She was thinking about the two of them and what they'd become. Where their relationship was bound.

"Well," he said, "maybe you ought to move in permanently."

Her heart soared as she realized that she hadn't been the only one to fall in love, and she leaned into him, drawing on his strength and warmth. Being one with him, as they'd been last night.

He hadn't actually voiced his thoughts in the way in which she'd hoped—flowers, candles and a little romance would have been nice—but his words had come from the heart.

She nudged him with her hip. "I thought you didn't get emotionally involved."

"I don't."

A chill of apprehension crept over her. "Then why do you want me to stay?" she asked, hoping he'd say the words she longed to hear. That he'd fallen in love with her, too.

"Because the baby needs you."

The earth tilted on its axis, and she struggled to right herself.

"And what about you?" she asked.

Clay tensed, but managed a smile. "What about me?"

"What do you want, Clay? What do you need?"

He paused for the longest time, her words stirring up all kinds of things. His first impulse had been to say that he was feeling something for her that he'd never felt before, but emotions were foreign to him and made him uneasy. On edge. Vulnerable.

There'd been a time, when he'd been a kid, that he'd had emotional needs. Like the kind a mother or father fulfilled. But he'd outgrown that, which was lucky. The needy guys were weak, and they couldn't tough it out when life threw an unexpected curve.

"I don't need anyone," he said.

And he didn't. Whenever he needed or wanted

anything, he bought it. But that didn't mean he didn't want Dani to stick around. She was good for the baby. And having the kids underfoot wasn't so bad. He was actually getting used to them.

"I see," she said. "You only want me to stay because of the baby."

He didn't see a problem with that. "I thought we had an understanding."

"What's that?"

He raked a hand through his hair. "That having sex would just be a one-night thing. It was nice. In fact, it was great. So I thought we could extend it indefinitely. If you decide to stay, I'd like you to share my bed."

For one brief, naked moment, she looked at him as though he'd jerked a welcome mat out from under her, but to be honest, it was far more than he'd offered any other woman. And last night, before he and Dani had made love, he never would have suggested it. But he could get used to loving her each night, to waking in her arms.

"You thought I could just move in and take care of the baby, huh?" She wore a pained expression that indicated she was more than annoyed, then she crossed her arms and shot him a wry smile. "And as a bonus, I get to sleep with you?"

Damn. He'd sensed something like this would happen. Women always changed after sex. Now Dani was getting all weird on him, too. Apparently, he hadn't expressed himself very well.

He wasn't good at this sort of thing, which was one reason he didn't get emotionally involved. He didn't like the turmoil or the drama.

"Listen, Dani. I like you—*a lot.* And I don't mind the kids being here, either." He brushed a strand of hair from her cheek and cast her a smile. "Stay. I'll make it worth your time."

She blinked, then her eyes widened, anger sparking. "Are you offering me money?" Her voice reached a decibel level he wasn't used to from her. "What do you think I am? A prostitute?"

Hell, no. Where had that come from?

"Of course not. I was just letting you know I'd put my money where my mouth was."

"The hell you will. And you can forget about all the places your mouth was last night."

"I didn't mean to upset you. I wasn't implying…"

"Maybe you ought to just leave a thousand dollars on the nightstand, and we'll call it even."

"That would mean…"

"Bingo."

"You're mad."

"I'm furious. Crushed. And hurt." She turned toward the door. "I'm going to shower, then pack. When the kids get home, we're leaving."

"What am I supposed to do without you?" he asked.

"For one thing, I suggest you change that baby's diapers. She's going to float out of them if you don't."

Then she turned and stormed away.

Leaving him hanging, dangling by his fingers.
And with no one to call on for help.

All the way home, the kids whined and voiced
their complaints about leaving the ranch sooner than
expected and while Toby and Kendra were still
visiting.

"Why did you make us go?" Marcos asked, tears
streaming down his face. "We love the ranch."

"And we love Angela and Hawk and Mr. Callaghan, too," Delia added.

Dani could certainly relate, but she refused to
take on the job of Clay's mistress and nanny. She
wanted love and marriage. And she couldn't tiptoe
around that house any longer, not after what they'd
shared last night, not after learning that Clay thought
her love and *services* could be bought.

"I don't understand why we couldn't at least stay
for dinner," Marcos said. "Hawk was going to make
hamburgers. And besides, Mr. Callaghan said we
weren't going home until at least Saturday."

Dani wasn't about to discuss her reasons with the
kids, even if she'd wanted to. She glanced across the
seat at Sara, wishing the girl were old enough to be
a confidante. Old enough to listen as Dani poured
out her heart and troubles. Old enough to offer some
advice or support.

"What about Bluebonnet?" Sara asked. "She's
going to miss me and think I abandoned her."

That horse had been good for Sara.

Dani opened her mouth to say something, to try to make her sister's disappointment easier to bear, but she couldn't think of a single word that might help. If she could, she'd comfort herself.

Instead, she tamped down her own feelings— like usual. But as her lip quivered and her eyes filled with tears, she realized the ploy wasn't working as well today.

The younger children were in the back seat, so they probably didn't suspect that Dani felt compelled to pull over on the side of the road and sob until the pain eased. She cast a surreptitious glance at Sara, only to meet a knowing gaze in the eyes of her younger sister. Sara obviously sensed that Dani was falling apart, but at least she had the courtesy not to bring it up or ask any questions.

As usual, Dani would suck it up and face her problems alone.

Oh, God. How could she have been so stupid?

She'd known better than to get involved with Clay. Now she feared he would follow through with his threat to find another firm to represent him, which would probably give Martin reason to believe that Dani hadn't behaved in a professional manner. And rightfully so.

Hadn't she started out by getting drunk on the plane and then ended up sleeping with the client?

How was that for going out with a bang?

A poor attempt at sarcastic humor failed miserably, and a tear slipped down her cheek. She swiped it away, only to have it replaced by another.

What was wrong with her? She was losing it for no reason.

Even if Clay was in touch with his feelings and the kind of man who wanted to settle down, she couldn't imagine herself on a ranch with a cowboy and raising a passel of young'uns. So how could she possibly think she'd fallen in love with him? They'd merely had sex. And somehow, over the course of several orgasms, she'd convinced herself that what they'd shared was real. And special.

That love had developed.

Why, it was merely her hormones and emotions playing a trick on her. That's all.

Oh, yeah? a small voice countered. So why do you feel like crying your eyes out?

Because when push came to shove, she couldn't downplay the fact that she'd offered Clay her heart and he'd broken it upon contact.

As they pulled into the driveway, Dani shut off the engine and handed Marcos the keys. "Why don't you unlock the door and take your things inside. I need to sit here for a while."

"Whatever," he said, grumbling under his breath.

Delia merely exited the car quietly, clutching her doll.

Sara, on the other hand, didn't make any effort to

move. And when the two of them were alone, she finally spoke. "What happened back there?"

Dani didn't know what to say. Certainly not the truth.

"I know you think of me as just a kid," Sara said. "But I'm a good friend. All my girlfriends come to me for advice. If you decided to confide in me, I might surprise you."

A bittersweet grin pulled at Dani's lips. "I really don't want to go into details, but…"

"But what?" Sara, with her long dark hair woven in a single braid down her back, suddenly looked older and wiser than her years.

"I, uh, have developed feelings…that are inappropriate…and—"

"Oh, God," Sara said. "I knew that would happen."

"What would happen?"

"That you'd fall in love with Mr. Callaghan. He's a real hunk. That is, for an old man."

He's not that old, Dani wanted to say in his defense.

"So what happened?" Sara asked. "Did you tell him how you felt?"

Dani took a deep breath, then blew it out. "No. He doesn't get emotionally attached."

"That's dumb," the girl said.

Yeah, well in Clay's case, it was also true.

"He might not *think* he gets attached," Sara added. "But he does."

"Why do you say that?"

"Because I've seen him with the dogs and the horses. He's got a heart for animals. And even though he doesn't like to hold Angela, he's always looking at her and checking her out. He talks to her, too. A man who doesn't care about kids just ignores them. And he doesn't give them horses, either." Sara grinned. "He's going to let me keep Bluebonnet at the ranch. Hawk told me."

Dani didn't mention that Clay might renege on the offer if she and the kids didn't live on the ranch. "You know, just because he cares about animals and others doesn't mean he can fall in love or make a lifetime commitment to a woman."

"Maybe he's just afraid to."

"Maybe. But a lot of good that does me."

"There are a ton of other guys out there," Sara said. "Men who would be happy to have you."

But how many would be willing to take on the care and raising of three children? Not so many, she suspected. But Dani appreciated the sentiment.

"And you know what?" Sara asked.

"What's that?"

"It's Mr. Callaghan's loss. He let the best thing in the world slip out of his hands."

Dani slid the girl a smile. "Thanks, Sara. Your friends are lucky to have you. And so am I."

As they climbed from the car and headed for the

house, Dani slipped an arm around her sister. For the first time in months Sara didn't pull away.

After their emotional confrontation, Clay knew there'd been no stopping Dani from leaving the ranch. And no chance of compromise. When Hawk and the kids returned from camping, she'd been packed and ready to leave.

"I don't know what you want me to do," he'd told her. "Or what more I can say."

"Not a thing." Then she climbed behind the wheel, taking three unhappy children with her.

As the dust kicked up behind her car, making it hard to see her disappearing taillights, Clay struggled with an ache in his chest the size of the Grand Canyon.

Four hours later, after the sun set over the ranch, he was still battling it.

When Dani left, she'd taken something away from him, and the loss was staggering.

Of course, he'd ignored his emotions for so long that he wasn't sure what was going on inside of him.

But how could she flip like that?

The night before, she'd agreed to have a purely sexual encounter. And all the while they'd made love—going through five condoms, mind you—there hadn't been any clue that things had changed. Then dawn broke, and he'd awakened with a completely new woman. One apparently looking for more than he could give her.

What had she wanted him to say?

That he loved her?

Hell, he wasn't sure he even knew what love was. As far as he was concerned, the word was overrated. It was a good heart that mattered.

He'd opened his home to Dani and her family. That ought to be enough to show her he cared and that she could depend on him to provide for her.

Clay turned on the television and surfed through the channels, but couldn't find anything to tweak his interest. Instead, he continued to ponder his feelings and considered going to Dani's house to admit that he might need her as much as the baby did.

Maybe that would be enough to sway her.

Outside, the dogs barked. Moments later a knock sounded, followed by the doorbell.

When he opened the door, Sara stood sheepishly on the porch.

He glanced out into the drive, not seeing a car of any kind. "How did you get here?"

She smiled sweetly. "I hitchhiked."

"Are you crazy? That's dangerous. You could have been hurt. Or abducted…" Or any number of terrible things.

The thought of something happening to Sara turned a knot in his gut.

"Don't stress, Mr. C. I just meant that I caught a ride with a friend. I'm not dumb." She grinned. "Can I come in?"

"Sure," he said, stepping aside. "But what are you doing here?"

"I came to tell you that I missed you. And that I wish we could all live at the ranch again."

He'd like that, too, but didn't see any need in telling her.

"Does your sister know you're here?" he asked, assuming she didn't.

"No. She'd probably be embarrassed."

"Why is that?"

"Because I want to ask you something."

Uh-oh. Why did he feel as though he ought to brace himself? "What do you want to know?"

"Do you care about my sister?"

Whoa. He wasn't so sure he wanted to admit it. But as the teenager peered at him with those big brown eyes, he shrugged. "Yeah. I care about her."

"How much?"

Enough to make him mope around like a lovesick puppy after she left. Enough for him to hate the peace and quiet he'd once looked forward to. "Quite a bit, I suppose."

"Do you love her? Even a little?"

Now the kid was going too far. Digging too deep. "I don't know."

She plopped down on the ottoman. "Do you love this ranch?"

He hadn't been especially partial to it when Rex had brought him here. But he'd grown to care about it—a lot. Enough to make something out of it. "I suppose I've gotten attached to it."

"And what about Mutt and Jeff and the puppies?"

"They're dogs."

"I love Bluebonnet," she said. "And she's a horse."

"What's your point?"

"I guess it's that you don't just love stuff or people right away. But sometimes true love grows. Know what I mean?"

Maybe so. He'd grown to care about Rex. And vice versa. But they'd never told each other. They'd never had to.

"Do you think you could grow to love Dani?" she asked.

He was beginning to suspect that's what was happening inside. That whatever he was feeling would only get stronger.

"Does it matter?" he asked.

"Heck, yes, it matters. A woman wants to know she has a place in a man's heart. A permanent place."

Yeah, well that place was now empty as hell.

"Okay. So she's wormed her way into my heart. And she's still burrowing."

"Then tell her."

He couldn't understand what all the hoopla was, about words and vows and commitments. "I offered her all I had to give, but it wasn't enough."

"You offered her *stuff*." She spit out the word

like it was cough medicine. "And stuff wears out and fades and all of that."

His money and his influence had always been enough in the past.

Except with Trevor.

"I just want more of your time," he'd once told Clay. "I want to know that I matter."

Damn. Had Clay screwed up again?

Was he going to lose someone else before having the chance to tell that someone how much he loved her?

The kids and Dani had brought something special to his life. They'd made him feel as though he mattered.

Especially Dani.

Damn. He really did love her.

And he was going to have to tell her.

"Come on," he told Sara. "We're going into town. I've got to talk to your sister."

Forty-five minutes later, Clay pulled along the curb in front of Dani's house. He unpacked Angela from the car seat and carried her to the front door.

Sara led the way, and Clay followed her inside.

Dani gasped and looked up from the lamp table, where she stood with a telephone in her hand.

A flood of emotion crossed her face. Surprise at seeing Clay, he supposed. And relief that Sara was home.

Dani returned the receiver into the cradle. "Sara,

where have you been? I've been worried sick. None of your friends knew where you were. I was just about to call the police and report you missing."

"She came out to the ranch," Clay said, rocking Angela in his arms, glad he had something—or someone—to hold on to.

"Thanks for bringing her home," Dani said, brushing her palms against her hips.

Clay cleared his throat, struggling with the words, then deciding to lay his heart on the line. "I haven't said this to anyone in ages. But I love you, Dani."

Her eyes locked on his, and her lips parted. Her expression seemed to flit between hope and skepticism. "Are you just saying that to get me to come back to the ranch?"

"I'm saying it because it's true. And if confronting my feelings and sharing them is what it'll take to get you to come home with me, then I will."

She glanced at Angela, who lay in his arm.

"Yes, I'll say it again. The baby needs you." He turned and handed Angela to Sara. "But I'm going to need you long after she grows up and leaves home."

Then he strode toward Dani, taking her hands in his. "I love you. Marry me. Live on the ranch."

An inner struggle played out on her face. "What about my job in town?"

"We'll have a nanny to look after the kids, and you can pursue your career."

"You wouldn't mind?" she asked. "It's a bit of a commute, so you'd be around the kids more often than I would."

"As long as you're in my bed each night—or most every night—I'll be a happy man."

"Then yes, Clay. I'll come back to the ranch with you."

His heart swelled in his chest, forcing out any fear of apprehension.

"Uh-oh," she said. "I just remembered I have a date on Saturday night."

Damn. He'd forgotten about that. His first impulse was to tell her to pick up the phone and cancel right now, but something told him he was going to have to use a more diplomatic approach with Dani. "I don't suppose you're still planning on going out."

"I most certainly am." Her words twisted a knot in his gut, then she tossed him a smile that quickly unraveled it. "But not with Brian. I think you and I have something to celebrate."

Clay pulled her close, his heart bursting with love. "For what it's worth, honey, I'll marry you as soon as we can pull if off."

"There's no rush," she said. "It's enough to know that you love me. And that you're willing to give our relationship a try. Besides, something tells me we'll have some adjustments to make."

"I'm sure we will. But marriage isn't nearly as

scary as I once thought. I'm looking forward to making a family with you."

"I love you, Clay." She wrapped her arms around his neck and kissed him with total abandon.

As the kids cheered, she slowly pulled her lips away from his but didn't step out of his embrace. "I love my job and I want to succeed with the firm. But I want to create a home, too. Somehow we'll make it work, blending hearts and lives. With your support, I'll balance family and career."

"Well, you've certainly put a nice balance back in my life." Clay turned to the kids, to his new family. "Come on, you guys. Go get packed. We're going home."

Then he stole another kiss from Dani, the woman who made him believe in the beauty and power of love.

And love, Clay realized, was more valuable than all the gold in Texas.

* * * * *

*Experience entertaining women's fiction
about rediscovery and reconnection—warm,
compelling stories that are relevant
for every woman who has wondered
"What's next?" in their lives.
After all, there's the life you planned.
And there's what comes next.*

*Turn the page for a sneak preview
of a new book from Harlequin NEXT.*

CONFESSIONS OF A NOT-SO-DEAD LIBIDO
by Peggy Webb

*On sale November 2006,
wherever books are sold.*

My husband could see beauty in a mud puddle. Literally. "Look at that, Louise," he'd say after a heavy spring rain. "Have you ever seen so many amazing colors in mud?"

I'd look and see nothing except brown, but he'd pick up a stick and swirl the mud till the colors of the earth emerged, and all of a sudden I'd see the world through his eyes—extraordinary instead of mundane.

Roy was my mirror to life. Four years ago when he died, it cracked wide open, and I've been living a smashed-up, sleepwalking life ever since.

If he were here on this balmy August night I'd

be sailing with him instead of baking cheese straws in preparation for Tuesday-night quilting club with Patsy. I'd be striving for sex appeal in Bermuda shorts and bare-toed sandals instead of opting for comfort in walking shoes and a twill skirt with enough elastic around the waist to make allowances for two helpings of lemon-cream pie.

Not that I mind Patsy. Just the opposite. I love her. She's the only person besides Roy who creates wonder wherever she goes. (She creates mayhem, too, but we won't get into that.) She's my mirror now, as well as my compass.

Of course, I have my daughter, Diana, but I refuse to be the kind of mother who defines herself through her children. Besides, she has her own life now, a husband and a baby on the way.

I slide the last cheese straws into the oven and then go into my office and open e-mail.

From: "Miss Sass" <patsyleslie@hotmail.com>
To: "The Lady" <louisejernigan@yahoo.com>
Sent: Tuesday, August 15, 6:00 PM
Subject: Dangerous Tonight
Hey Lady,

I'm feeling dangerous tonight. Hot to trot, if you know what I mean. Or can you even remember?☺ Look out, bridge club, here I come. I'm liable to end up dancing on the tables instead of bidding

three spades. Whose turn is it to drive, anyhow?
Mine or thine?
XOXOX
Patsy
P.S. Lord, how did we end up in a club with no
men?

This e-mail is typical "Patsy." She's the only
person I know who makes me laugh all the time. I
guess that's why I e-mail her about ten times a day.
She lives right next door, but e-mail satisfies my
urge to be instantly and constantly in touch with
her without having to interrupt the flow of my life.
Sometimes we even save the good stuff for e-mail.

From: "The Lady" <louisejernigan@yahoo.com>
To: "Miss Sass" <patsyleslie@hotmail.com>
Sent: Tuesday, August 15, 6:10 PM
Subject: Re: Dangerous Tonight
So, what else is new, Miss Sass? You're always
dangerous. If you had a weapon, you'd be
lethal.☺
Hugs,
Louise
P.S. What's this about men? I thought you said
your libido was dead?

I press Send then wait. Her reply is almost instan-
taneous.

From: "Miss Sass" <patsyleslie@hotmail.com>
To: "The Lady" <louisejernigan@yahoo.com>
Sent: Tuesday, August 15, 6:12 PM
Subject: Re: Dangerous Tonight
Ha! If I had a *brain* I'd be lethal.
And I said my libido was in hibernation, not DEAD!
Jeez, Louise!!!!!
P

Patsy loves to have the last word, so I shut off my computer.

* * * * *

Want to find out what happens to their friendship when Patsy and Louise both find the perfect man?

Don't miss
CONFESSIONS OF A NOT-SO-DEAD LIBIDO
by Peggy Webb,

*coming to Harlequin NEXT
in November 2006.*

HARLEQUIN®

Next™

Entertaining women's fiction for every woman who has wondered "what's next?" in her life.

Receive $1.⁰⁰ off

any Harlequin NEXT™ novel.

Coupon expires March 31, 2007.
Redeemable at participating retail outlets
in the U.S. only. Limit one coupon per customer.

5 65373 00076 2   (8100) 0 11266

HARLEQUIN®

Next™

**Entertaining women's fiction
for every woman who has
wondered "what's next?"
in her life.**

Receive $1.⁰⁰ off

any Harlequin NEXT™ novel.

Coupon expires March 31, 2007.
Redeemable at participating retail outlets
in Canada only. Limit one coupon per customer.

52607178

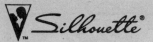

Silhouette®
Romantic
SUSPENSE

INTIMATE MOMENTS™

Excitement, danger and passion guaranteed

Beginning in October
Silhouette Intimate Moments®
will be evolving into
Silhouette® Romantic Suspense.

Look for it wherever you buy books!

REQUEST YOUR FREE BOOKS!

2 FREE NOVELS PLUS 2 FREE GIFTS!

▼ Silhouette®

SPECIAL EDITION™

Life, Love and Family!

YES! Please send me 2 FREE Silhouette Special Edition® novels and my 2 FREE gifts. After receiving them, if I don't wish to receive any more books, I can return the shipping statement marked "cancel." If I don't cancel, I will receive 6 brand-new novels every month and be billed just $4.24 per book in the U.S., or $4.99 per book in Canada, plus 25¢ shipping and handling per book and applicable taxes, if any*. That's a savings of at least 15% off the cover price! I understand that accepting the 2 free books and gifts places me under no obligation to buy anything. I can always return a shipment and cancel at any time. Even if I never buy another book from Silhouette, the two free books and gifts are mine to keep forever.

235 SDN EEYU   335 SDN EEY6

Name   (PLEASE PRINT)

Address   Apt.

City   State/Prov.   Zip/Postal Code

Signature (if under 18, a parent or guardian must sign)

Mail to Silhouette Reader Service™:

IN U.S.A.
P.O. Box 1867
Buffalo, NY
14240-1867

IN CANADA
P.O. Box 609
Fort Erie, Ontario
L2A 5X3

Not valid to current Silhouette Special Edition subscribers.

Want to try two free books from another line?
Call 1-800-873-8635 or visit www.morefreebooks.com.

* Terms and prices subject to change without notice. NY residents add applicable sales tax. Canadian residents will be charged applicable provincial taxes and GST. This offer is limited to one order per household. All orders subject to approval. Credit or debit balances in a customer's account(s) may be offset by any other outstanding balance owed by or to the customer. Please allow 4 to 6 weeks for delivery.

SSE06

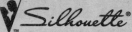

SSECNM1006